Emma Clarke Pratt
ONE LIFE

A novel by
Marjorie Irish Randell

ISBN: 978-1-4907-7256-1 (sc)
ISBN: 978-1-4907-7254-7 (hc)
ISBN: 978-1-4907-7255-4 (e)

Library of Congress Control Number: 2016906349

Trafford rev.   04/28/2016

 www.trafford.com

North America & international
toll-free: 1 888 232 4444 (USA & Canada)
fax: 812 355 4082

Foreword

This book is based on facts gleaned from stories remembered by the family, diaries kept faithfully by George Hazen Pratt, letters from George Hazen Pratt to Emma and facts verified by avid genealogist George Milton Randell, my brother-in-law.

Dialogue and everyday happenings I have imagined, hoping to add interest to Emma's story. Emma was a very special forward-thinking young woman for her time in the late 1800's, and I believe her story is well worth recording for posterity.

_____Marjorie Irish Randell

The Pratt Family Motto

"Judicium-Parium-Aut-Lex-Terre"

when translated, becomes

"Rule The Land With Equal Justice"

Chapter One

*E*mma Clarke was running as fast as her six-year-old legs would carry her. At last she reached the edge of the trees that harbored her secret place. Once she saw the banks of the little creek she flung herself down on the ground, panting and sobbing.

"Why do we have to go? Why can't we just stay right here," she begged of an invisible someone. Gradually the sobbing subsided as the quietness of the woods soothed her. The sound of water on the nearby rocks came through to her and she rolled over on her back to look up through the leaves at the bright blue July sky of Ohio. Kansas seemed half a world away when Papa and Mama talked about it. Would there be woods there? Emma hated the thought of moving. She wanted to stay right there. As she unbuttoned her high-top shoes and pulled off her long black stockings her anxiety faded. The cold, clear water made her shiver, but she gathered up her skirts and splashed in the shallow, sandy-bottomed creek. The sun was casting long shadows before Emma remembered that she hadn't told anyone where she was going. She sat on a rock struggling to get her stockings back on wet feet when she heard her older sister Elizabeth calling.

"Emma! Emma! Suppertime. Where are you? Emma!" Elizabeth's voice was closer with each word. "Oh Emma, for goodness sake! I thought you might be here. Hurry. Get your shoes and stockings on! You don't want to be late for supper. Papa is coming home tonight."

"I know he's coming."

"Tomorrow we start on our big trip, remember, and we must get the rest of our things packed," Elizabeth said as she bent over to help Emma fasten the last buttons on her shoes.

"I don't want to go," Emma said stoutly, her lower lip extending ever so slightly, her head down.

"Come on, Emma, we have to go. Papa and Mama have decided and we have to go."

"I know, but I don't want to."

Elizabeth took Emma's hand as the two little girls started out of the woods toward the group of houses where they lived.

"Mama wants you to watch Dillyshane while she finishes supper. Better hurry. I think we can find woods in Kansas, too, Emma. Try to think of the good things. Mamma needs us and it's easier for her if we're happy about going,"

Elizabeth was just two years older than Emma but because she was the oldest of the three children her attitude toward Emma was maternal. Somehow, after Elizabeth's words Emma didn't feel quite as bad as she had about going. Maybe . . .

The next morning the girls were awakened while the sky outside their window was still dark.

"Hurry and get dressed, girls. This is the day of the beginning of our big trip to Kansas. Remember? We will soon get to see Grandpa and Grandma Lacey."

The girls pulled on their clothes, including the long black stockings and their high-buttoned shoes. Their mother was folding the blankets that made up their beds. Little brother Dillyshane who whimpered at being awakened so early, resorted to sucking his thumb after his mother pulled his clothes on over his head.

"There is bread for your breakfast. Be sure to finish your milk. We may not have fresh milk every day while we're traveling."

The children, still sleepy, ate the thick slices of bread their mother had cut and spread generously with butter. By the time the bread and milk was gone they were fully awake and anxious to get up into the big wagon.

"Elizabeth, help me with this bundle, will you?" Elizabeth at eight years old was enlisted for helping her mother. Even Emma carried small last minute things out to her father who hoisted her up into the wagon to stow the things away.

Thomas, with dark hair and a full, long beard, was a tall man, slender and, Emma thought, handsome. She was proud of her papa and always tried to please him and do as he asked. Thomas smiled at her now as she continued bringing the last minute items to be stowed up inside the big wagon.

At last all was loaded and all three children were up in the huge wagon that was filled with all of their belongings. Last up was their mother Francis. She was still tying her bonnet as father Thomas urged the horses to begin pulling the heavily laden wagon. It was a hard pull . . . a real struggle for them to get started but once the big wagon was in motion the load eased for the four horses. The morning sun was coloring the eastern sky gold with deep shades of pink as they pulled away.

Chapter Two

*F*rancis's parents . . . the Laceys . . . had, the year before, moved from Pataskala, Ohio asking their son-in-law Thomas Clarke to sell the farm for them. It had taken nearly a year to do that and now, of course, Francis wanted so much to be nearer her parents. As a lawyer Thomas felt he could find work wherever they might live and had agreed to pack up and follow Francis's parents to Kansas. He bought the huge wooden wagon and fashioned the curved wooden staves that now were covered with the white cotton canvas Francis cut and stitched to fit, making a snug interior for their big wagon.

Even Emma had, at last, to admit that it was an adventure to be up in the huge wagon. Her blues of the day before were receding as the three children bounced along inside the wagon amidst all the household belongings of the family. The girls giggled together and Elizabeth said, "See, Emma! It's fun! I know you will find trees and a creek in Kansas, too." She turned her attention to Dillyshane and began playing patty-cake with him, laughing and singing. Emma smiled. Elizabeth was right.

It was fun.

Later along the way Emma finally confided in Elizabeth by whispering in her ear, "It is fun, Elizabeth. I never thought it would be."

"A covered wagon is different, isn't it?"

"Oh yes, Elizabeth, it is. Even when Papa was building it I just couldn't imagine it would be such fun. We can even peek out the back.

Will Papa let us walk outside sometimes like Mama does?" Emma asked.

"I don't know. We'll just have to ask him, I think. We may have to run, not walk, though, in order to keep up." Elizabeth laughed at the expression on Emma's face at the mention of running. "We used to run all the time in Ohio."

"But this is a dusty old trail, not a green grassy place," Emma pouted.

"Come on, Emma. Cheer up. We are a couple of really lucky girls. It isn't everyone that has such a nice big covered wagon to ride in . . . or walk beside."

"Who will look after Dillyshane** if we walk outside?" Emma asked.

---

*   Dillyshane is an Irish name meaning 'Last of the lot.'

"Mama will probably come back here to stay with him. Shall we climb over things and go ask Papa now if we can do it?" Elizabeth grinned at her little sister.

"All right by me . . . if you think he'll say yes!" The two girls clamored over the household goods they had carefully packed so there was a certain way to get up to the front of the wagon without harming anything.

"Papa . . . Papa, we need to talk to you!" Emma gasped before Thomas was even aware the girls were near the front of the wagon.

"Yes, Papa, we want to ask you something." Elizabeth said, smiling at her father.

"All right. Ask away." Thomas half turned around to see the girls. "Something important?"

"Yes, we think so." Elizabeth said.

"Yes, Papa, it's important . . . real important, we think." Emma pulled herself up toward Thomas. "Can Elizabeth and I walk beside the wagon like Mama does sometimes?" Both girls watched their father anxiously.

"Well, let's see now. Do you have a measuring stick?" Thomas was looking very serious as he questioned the girls.

"Why in the world would we need a measuring stick, Papa?" Elizabeth asked.

"Well . . ." Thomas still held his serious expression. "It will take someone with long legs to keep walking as fast as these horses do. We need to measure your legs to see if they're long enough."

Emma dropped her head.

"There is no way our legs could be as long as Mama's are," she said sadly.

"I told you we might have to run and not walk." Elizabeth looked as disappointed as Emma did.

Thomas turned around to see the girls' expressions.

"Elizabeth is right, Emma. If you want to be outside you would probably have to run to keep up."

Thomas was finding it hard to turn down his girls' request. Suddenly he broke out into a big grin, "But . . . let's have you try it next time we stop for a rest. You girls can get outside then and your mama can come in with Dillyshane. Remember though, it will be tough going for you until we stop again. You'll get tired . . . real tired."

Emma and Elizabeth clapped their hands and laughed and giggled.

"Oh, thank you, Papa!" Emma called as she began scrambling back across their possessions. "We won't get tired, I know. It's going to be fun, fun, fun."

Elizabeth joined Emma further back in the wagon and the girls began playing their patty-cake games again . . . this time with lots of smiles and laughter, both of them happy with anticipation.

It was almost an hour before Thomas stopped the horses for a rest and a long drink of water. The girls jumped down from the high wagon, calling out to their mother.

"Mama! Mama! Papa says we can walk outside and you can ride inside with Dillyshane! We're so excited!"

Francis looked up at Thomas. "Are you sure, Thomas? Those horses move right along and it has me almost running to keep up."

"I told them they had to have long legs to do that or else they would be running." He had hopped down from the wagon seat and was filling a bucket of water from the big barrel roped to the side of the wagon.

"But you can't keep stopping the horses to let the girls climb up again, Thomas."

"I know." As Francis came up to be near him he confided quietly, "I thought this was the only way for them to learn first hand. They will be two tired little girls tonight."

"If you're sure . . ."

Francis could hear Dillyshane's whimpers becoming more like cries as she climbed up into the wagon. "Your mama is here, Dillyshane. I'm coming. I'm coming."

The girls played tag around the wagon while their father watered each of the four horses. Finally they were ready to start again.

"Ready, girls?" Thomas climbed up onto the wagon seat.

"Be sure to keep up now. We don't want to lose you two." He gave his little click-click sound to get the horses started and the wagon began rolling ahead.

Emma and Elizabeth laughed with excitement and began walking alongside the wagon as it started. When it gained momentum the girls soon found they were behind the wagon instead of alongside. In no time at all they began to run in order to keep up.

"I guess Papa was right," Elizabeth called to Emma.

"I guess . . . " Emma returned, grinning.

It was only after about half an hour that the girls were not able to keep up and were further and further behind the wagon. Their running was becoming slower and was hard work.

Francis peered out the back opening of the wagon. "Come on girls. You're too far back there. Come on . . . we don't want to have to stop the horses again yet. Elizabeth! Emma! Come on! Faster! Run!"

Needless to say, both girls fell asleep that evening, before either Dillyshane or their parents could say goodnight to them. To walk and run behind the covered wagon was a lot more exercise than they had thought it would be.

By the next night they had grown more used to trading off running time and the care of Dillyshane with their mother. They were even able to scurry around the area where they stopped for the night to find wood for the campfire their father built. It was nearly dark by the time they had all finished their supper and the girls had cleaned their metal plates with sand.

The traveling from Ohio to Kansas in a covered wagon was a great adventure for the children. Stopping at night and cooking their supper over the fire Papa built was so different from anything they had ever known before. Sleeping in the wagon was definitely not like sleeping in their beds back in Ohio. Emma put her head outside of the wagon before they went to sleep.

"There are a million stars out there in the sky, 'Lizbeth," she said as she settled down into the blankets.

"I know. I peeked outside, too. So many of them and they all sparkle like little diamonds. For some reason, there seem to be many, many more stars in the sky as we travel along than there were back at home." Elizabeth snuggled up closer to Emma and reached out to make sure Dillyshane was covered well. He was already asleep and had been for an hour at least. "We need to go to sleep, Emma. Close your eyes and say your prayers. You will be asleep before you know it."

Thomas and Francis had been asleep for as long as Dillyshane. They were exhausted. Francis walked beside the wagon for long periods during the day and Thomas found it tiring work to drive the four-horse team it took to pull their heavily loaded wagon. Because both Emma and Elizabeth had walked and run alongside the wagon that day they were soon joining them.

Thomas Dowling Clarke

Chapter Three

*B*efore long the days became much the same and everyone was happy to see, many days later, the outskirts of newly settled Kansas City come into view. Emma's parents were exhausted when they reached the city and were willing to settle down and stay for what the girls hoped would be for quite some time . . . this time.

Thomas hung out his shingle and was, thankfully, very busy writing up deeds, wills and deeds of sale, making money with his lawyer work. Emma and Elizabeth were enrolled in school and in the summer Elizabeth even found shade trees along the bank of a small stream that Thomas told them was a "tributary of the big Missouri river."

"What's a tributary, Elizabeth?" Emma asked as she unbuttoned her high-top shoes.

"I think it means a branch of the river."

"Why didn't he just say 'branch' then, I wonder." She pulled off her long black stockings.

"Oh, Papa just likes to use his lawyer words, I think. Maybe it's his way of teaching us, too. You learned something today by his saying that, didn't you?" Elizabeth smiled knowingly.

"Yes, I guess I did. A tributary of a big river is a branch of a big river. Right?" Emma laughed as she dipped her toes into the cold water.

The two girls waded cautiously in the water at the edges, being careful not to go out into the stream. Thomas had cautioned them as one could never tell how deep the water might be in the middle, nor how fast the current might be. 'Better to be safe than sorry,' he had told them.

It was fun, though, even at the edges and they were soon fairly wet over most of their clothing. They had been giggling and splashing for quite a while when they noticed the sun was beginning to touch down in the west. They hurriedly tugged on the black stockings, pulled on their shoes and started running toward home without even attempting to button them.

"What is Mama going to say when she sees our wet clothes?" Emma panted as they ran.

"I expect we will get a scolding."

"Oh dear."

Elizabeth was right. They did get a scolding before they were dunked in a tub of hot water and scrubbed, then put into nightclothes and sent to bed without any supper.

The two girls shared a bed. They were drifting off to sleep when Elizabeth, unexpectedly, sat up. "Emma . . . Emma . . . I just thought of something," she whispered.

Emma moaned.

"Remember when we were back in Ohio," Elizabeth asked. "And you were worrying if there would be a stream of water and trees in Kansas like we had in Ohio?"

Another moan.

"Emma! Don't you remember? You have to remember."

"Yes, I remember," Emma mumbled. "You're waking me up . . . and I was having a nice dream."

"Sorry. But Emma, you have to remember so that you can understand. All your worries were for nothing. We have a stream of water and we have trees . . . right here in Kansas City."

"I remember, 'Lizbeth. I won't worry any more. Now . . . can I go back to sleep?"

Elizabeth settled back down in bed once more and snuggled up close to Emma beneath the covers. "I can sleep now, too. 'Night, Emma."

But Emma was already in dreamland.

The very next evening as the girls sat around the table with their parents eating supper together, Thomas cleared his throat before beginning to talk.

"Listen, everyone. I have an announcement to make."

The girls looked around. Everyone? It was just the two of them and their mother. Dillyshane had already been put to bed. The girls did turn toward their father, though, to give him their undivided attention.

When the three had laid down their forks and looked toward Thomas he smiled broadly.

"You know your Lacey grandparents have decided to move on again. This time it's all the way to California. They're going on the train by way of Salt Lake City, Utah."

Yes, of course they knew. But they had both forgotten exactly what that would mean for them.

The girls' mother resumed eating and only smiled a bit at the girls. Francis knew, of course, what was coming next.

"I have managed to sell your grandparents' house, as well as ours, very, very quickly. It's hard to believe. We must be out of our house by this time two weeks from today."

Both girls groaned. Elizabeth voiced their feelings, "Not again, Daddy! We're just nicely settled."

"We finally found a stream bed and some trees like in Ohio just yesterday," Emma pleaded.

"Sorry, girls, but that's the way it has to be this time."

More groaning.

"There is something good about this time, though." Thomas waited for some reaction.

Elizabeth looked at him. "What can be good about it, Papa?"

"We will be traveling by train!" Thomas smiled. He was obviously proud of his ability to set up the surprise. "We will be riding on the new Transcontinental Railroad that just opened a year ago!"

"The new Transcontinental Railroad?" Elizabeth was the only one who seemed impressed.

"Yes, indeed," Thomas replied, as he resumed eating his dinner.

"We heard about that new railroad in school this year. It sounded really exciting then." Elizabeth turned to her sister. "Come on, Emma. Smile. We're going on a new adventure!"

"I don't want to go," Emma grumbled. "Why do we have to keep moving all the time? Can't we just let Grandpa and Grandma Lacey move to San Francisco without us this time?"

Thomas looked at Francis who began fussing with the edge of the tablecloth, refusing to look up and meet her husband's eyes.

Both girls knew exactly why they had to keep following the Lacey's wherever they went, but secretly they wanted their mother to admit it was her fault . . . that she felt she just couldn't be separated from her parents. They waited, along with Thomas, for several minutes. Finally Thomas looked at the girls.

"Girls, your mother wants to be close to her parents. I agreed quite a few years ago to follow along after them as they moved across the United States. I obtained a special license so that I could work anywhere we go in our travels. Besides . . . isn't it great fun to see all of this wonderful country we live in?"

"I like it right here," Emma said firmly.

"I'm ready to go, Papa!" Elizabeth's face was radiant with happiness.

"Perhaps you can influence your sister," Thomas smiled fondly at Elizabeth. "It would be nice to have two happy daughters."

That night as the girls crawled under the covers together Elizabeth said softly, "Tomorrow we leave, Emma. It's going to be fun. Really. Remember I told you that about the covered wagon before when you didn't want to go and what fun it turned out to be? Remember?"

Emma turned away from her sister as she mumbled, "I remember."

"Come on, then, Emma. Be happy. We're going on an adventure like I told you before. It's going to be a big adventure this time. We're going to be riding on a train!"

"What's so great about riding on a train?" Emma asked.

"Well . . . let's see . . . . It will be really, really different from anything we have ever done before, and . . . it will get us there sooner than we could have if we continued on with the wagon and horses . . . ."

Elizabeth seemed to be hesitating quite a while.

Emma prompted her, "And?"

"And . . . it will be loads of fun," she finished triumphantly.

"Good night, Elizabeth," Emma said as she pulled the covers over her head in an effort to stop any further conversation.

Chapter Four

*T*he next morning the girls were awakened as Dillyshane began pounding on the edge of their bed. He kept chanting, "Train ride. Train ride. Train ride."

For the first time ever he was up before Emma and Elizabeth.

"Go away, Dillyshane. Stop pounding on our bed. You're waking us up." Elizabeth gently pushed her little brother away from the bed.

"Papa says wake up . . . wake up," he declared.

"Dillyshane, go away," Emma groaned.

"Go ride train. Ride train n-o-w, Emmmmmma!"

Francis peeked around the corner just then. "He's right, girls. It's time to wake up and go for that train ride. Your Papa wants to leave right after breakfast. Come on. What Dillyshane says to you is right. Wake up. Wake up." Then as an after thought, "Papa needs to pack your bed. Come on. Up. Up." The girls tumbled out of bed.

Several hours later all of the Clarke family were aboard the big noisy railroad train. Elizabeth was as excited as Dillyshane and their mother. Thomas kept busy making sure all of their possessions and furniture had made it aboard with them, that they were in the right car of the train and that tickets were available for the conductor who would come through the car fairly soon after they started. Dillyshane was jumping up and down.

"Big train, big train. Train ride! Train ride! Train ride!"

Elizabeth hugged him. "We really are going for a train ride, aren't we, Dillyshane? Isn't this fun?"

Even Emma had become excited. "It is an adventure, Elizabeth. You were right. It's just as you said it would be."

Then she turned to Dillyshane, "Train ride! Train ride, Dilly! Train ride!"

The three children gradually became used to the novelty of riding on a train. They loved eating the picnic food Francis had packed in a basket before they left. Dillyshane continued assaulting them with his, "Train ride! Train ride!"

There were a few times when the train stopped to take on water. One time when they stopped Elizabeth was looking out the window and suddenly she poked Emma.

"Look, Emma! See those children? They're Indian! Let's get out and talk to them." Elizabeth was up from her seat, headed for the end of the car. "How can you talk to them? Can you speak 'Indian'?" Emma called as she got up and followed her sister out of the car.

The Indian children couldn't speak English but they could smile and hold out little leather purses and bookmarks they had made to sell.

"Did you make these?" Elizabeth asked one little boy. She pointed to a small purse and then pointed to the boy holding it. He nodded and held one out to Elizabeth. She looked it over carefully, peeking inside after loosening the leather drawstring. "How much?"

The Indian boy held up six fingers.

"Six pennies?"

The boy nodded again.

Elizabeth felt in the pocket of her sturdy denim dress and pulled out two pennies. Another dip into the pocket brought out three more making it a total of five. She reached in again. No more pennies. She looked at the Indian boy and held out the five pennies she had. He smiled shyly, took the pennies and handed Elizabeth the little leather drawstring purse.

"Oh, thank you! Thank you," she said.

Emma was looking at a little Indian girl who had smiled at her. Emma didn't have any pennies for buying a purse but she and the Indian girl began running around a couple of big rock boulders together, laughing as they ran.

"Come on, girls," Thomas called. "Time to climb back up into the train!"

The girls ran to their father and Thomas hoisted them up one at a time. They waved and called to their new Indian friends as the train resumed its journey toward California.

A few days later Elizabeth seemed content to just sit in a corner and not join in with her siblings in playing little games in the train compartment as they had before.

"Elizabeth, aren't you going to play games with your brother and sister?" Francis asked.

"I don't feel like it, Mama. I just want to sit here."

Francis put her hand on Elizabeth's forehead.

"You feel as if you might have a little fever."

Later Francis said, "Why don't you lie down here on the seat beside me?"

Elizabeth did as her mother suggested and seemed content to stay there the rest of the day.

The next morning when Francis felt of Elizabeth's forehead and cheeks she told Thomas, "She's burning up with fever." Thomas sat with his eldest daughter holding onto one of her feet and rubbing it as he read his paper. Later he read aloud to her from one of her books.

"Mama," Emma confided. "I think I'm getting hot like 'Lizbeth is."

Francis checked her with alarm. "You are feverish, Emma. Better lie down here on the other seat." Francis kept putting wet cold cloths on both girls' foreheads.

When the conductor came through the car he made a clucking sound out of the side of his mouth. "Looks like you've got some Scarlet Fever patients here. There's some other cases in the next car."

The train kept chugging along and was soon pulling into Ogden, Utah. The conductor came through making an announcement to everyone. "All Scarlet Fever cases must get off at the next stop. Next stop . . . Ogden, Utah. Coming up. Pack up your belongings. Prepare to get off the train."

Thomas found a porter to remove and carry their bags and possessions off the train while he carried Elizabeth in his arms. Francis carried Emma over her shoulder and took Dillyshane by the hand. It was a sorry group of Clarkes and other Scarlet Fever patients clustered on the station platform watching the train pull away without them.

Somehow Thomas managed to carry Elizabeth and give orders for their belongings, plus engaging a conveyance to take them to a hotel in Ogden. They put the girls to bed immediately and Thomas began his search for a doctor to come see the girls.

By the time the doctor arrived at their rooms in the hotel Elizabeth was not responding to her mother's careful nursing. She was again burning with fever, calling out in delirium. After numerous days she quieted. But it was an alarming quiet. The doctor came again, this time to shake his head.

"She won't last the night, I'm afraid."

Elizabeth died that night in Ogden.

Thomas was again scurrying about, this time to find an undertaker, and a place to bury their dear Elizabeth. He tucked the undertaker's receipt in his pocket, later putting it with his important papers.

Emma and Dillyshane were both ill with Scarlet Fever, too. Francis nursed them constantly, fearful that she might lose another child. Fortunately, the two younger children were not as severely stricken as their sister and they began to recover.

Francis called the children to breakfast one morning after Emma and Dillyshane seemed to be recovered from the dreaded fever. Dillyshane came running to climb up in his high chair calling out, "Brek-k-fust, Emma! Brek-k-fust!"

Emma, lying on the floor, kept on coloring with some crayons Thomas had managed to find for her. She turned the paper she had found this way and that to see which color looked best. She didn't seem to hear her brother.

Francis called, "Emma! Breakfast is ready! Come!"
Still there was no response from Emma.

Francis looked at her husband. "Thomas, she can't hear me."

Thomas looked up from his paper. "Try it again, Francis. Louder."

"Emma! Breakfast is ready. Come!"

Emma kept on coloring contentedly. Finally Francis touched her arm.

"Emma. Can you hear me?"

"What did you say, Mama? I can't hear you."

Thomas took Emma to see the doctor the next day, telling him about her not being able to hear them. Doctor tested and talked to Emma.

"She seems to have lost her hearing. It's from the Scarlet Fever, I think. It may only be temporary," he said. "Watch her closely and keep in touch with me. It may be just for a bit."

The days and weeks went by with Emma still not hearing them. Then one morning about six months later Thomas was talking to Francis. "Maybe we should take her to the doctor again."

"Why, Papa? Why take me to the doctor again?"

Francis and Thomas both turned toward her eagerly, "Emma?"

Emma sat up from the game she was playing. "Mama! I can hear! For so long I couldn't hear anything! But I heard you, Papa! I can even hear the crickets outside now!"

What a happy threesome they were dancing about in the living room. "Emma can hear! Emma can hear!" Even Dillyshane joined in the chanting.

"We have so much to be thankful for, Thomas. We've lost our dear Elizabeth, but we have Emma and Dillyshane. And now Emma can hear again! Dillyshane seems to have come through it all unscathed."

Thomas didn't say anything. He just took her hand, looked at her with tears in his eyes and nodded his head.

Chapter Five

*L*etters from the Laceys were filled with the wonders of San Francisco and the question of when the Clarkes would be coming on to join them there. For a time Thomas and Francis ignored the inquiries.

"It's almost impossible to go on and leave Elizabeth here." Francis sobbed.

"I know, dear. I know." He gathered her in his arms. "We will just have to carry her with us in our hearts. Carry her, and the many happy memories we have of her. We must think of Emma and Dillyshane now. We should get settled some place so they can go to school and know they will be staying there and not moving on again just after they've made new friends."

"You are right. I must try to remember. I know you, too, find it so very hard to leave Elizabeth here. But I will try, Thomas. I will try to remember to carry Elizabeth in my heart as you do . . . even though her body is here." She leaned into Thomas sobbing. He held her for quite some time, attempting to assuage her sorrow as well as his own.

Finally, the decision made, Thomas and Francis packed their things, made arrangements for their belongings to be sent to San Francisco and went one last time to say goodbye to Elizabeth in the cemetery. This time Emma and Dillyshane were with them.

"I don't want to leave Elizabeth here alone, Mama." Emma looked up into her mother's face and saw her mother's tears matching her own.

"Emma, we will carry Elizabeth always in our hearts. She will always and forever be with us." Francis choked back her sobs. "Try to remember."

Thomas picked up Dillyshane and took Emma's hand. "Come on, children. Your Lacey grandparents are waiting patiently for us in San Francisco. It's time for us to go."

The Clarkes had stayed on in Ogden, Utah for a year after Elizabeth's death. Even after a year, when they left it felt as if they had left part of themselves there.

And of course . . . they had.

The train ride from Ogden to San Francisco was a very exciting one, especially for Emma and

Dillyshane. They had never been in mountains as high as the Rocky Mountains. And rocky they were. Tunnels were chiseled out of the rocks to make way for the trains. Higher and higher they went. Emma peered out the windows of the train and looked straight down as they still kept climbing.

"Dilly . . . isn't this exciting? We're climbing up the side of the mountain!" Emma hugged Dillyshane like she had seen Elizabeth do. She wanted to be Elizabeth for him.

"Climb mow-tin. Climb mow-tin." He had started sucking his thumb again after Elizabeth had broken him of the habit. Emma couldn't let that happen.

"Come on, Dilly, let's press our noses to the window and find out how far down we can see!" Dillyshane pulled his thumb from his mouth and pressed his nose and both hands against the train car window. Emma smiled. Elizabeth would be pleased, she knew. She missed her sister more than she had let on to the family. She tried to imagine her still sitting with them on the train. It was tough going for Emma but it helped to become absorbed in caring for Dillyshane.

Thomas came to sit with the children.

"This is the Donner Pass. More than twenty years ago a group of people in covered wagons attempted to cross this pass and were stopped by the snow and lack of food. Many of them died."

"What a sad story, Papa," Emma said.

"Yes. Yes, it is sad. We are so fortunate to be able to ride in this big, comfortable train."

"And we have food, don't we, Papa? Mama packed us a wonderful basket of good things to eat," Emma smiled, knowingly. "Is it time for us to eat now, do you think?"

"Why don't we ask your mama?" Thomas turned toward his wife with a small smile. "Francis, Emma's wondering if it's time to eat."

"Are you sure it's Emma who's wondering?" Francis laughed at him.

"Me hon-gree, Mama! Me hon-gree!" Dillyshane chimed in.

"Well, well! I guess it must really be time to eat if Dillyshane thinks it's time." Francis reached for the basket of food she had prepared before they got on the train.

"There are corncakes, there are dried beef pieces and," she rummaged in the basket, "some cheese!"

The four Clarkes sat together in their compartment munching on the corncakes and chewing away at the beef pieces that Francis had cut into strips before drying them.

"We have eggs and potatoes and carrots but we need a fire to cook them," Francis told the children. "We can have those later when we stop and can build a fire."

'How long will it take us to get to San Francisco, Papa?" Emma asked.

"We'll probably be there in another day or so."

Francis's face lit up. "I hope my parents are still staying there."

"They usually wait for us to catch up with them before they move on," Thomas smiled at his wife.

"Let's hope they stay for awhile after we get there so we can really see something of them." Francis said.

The whole family dozed after the food remains were cleaned up and put away. They were unaware that the sun was going down. When Thomas stirred later and looked out the window it was completely black outside. He settled back then and joined the rest of his little family in sleep.

Chapter Six

*T*he Lacey's did wait until the Clarkes arrived in San Francisco. They seemed to be delighted when they heard the news that another baby was coming within a few months, but itchy feet prevailed and didn't keep them from moving on up to Seattle by ship before the big event.

Little Myra arrived several months later to the delight of Emma and Dillyshane. Emma loved playing "nursemaid" to the baby and Dillyshane danced about with shining eyes. "My-ra! My-ra," he would chant. He was happy to be playing the part of the proud older brother.

One morning as Francis and Thomas were lingering over second cups of coffee at the breakfast table Francis said, "I wish my parents could see this new little one, Thomas."

"Well, honey, they could have waited a few more months before they moved up to Seattle." Thomas resumed reading the morning paper.

Francis was quiet for a bit, looking thoughtful and pensive. After some time she began to smile, then reached across to grasp Thomas's arm.

"Thomas! I have a wonderful idea! Listen . . . Thomas! Put down that paper and listen to me!"

Thomas finally did as he was told. The paper was put down and he looked at Francis questioningly.

"I have this wonderful idea, Thomas!"

"All right. Let's hear it."

"Because my parents weren't here to see the new baby . . . I feel as if I should do something about it. So-o-o, Thomas . . ." Francis paused. "My idea is that I can take Myra on the ship up to Seattle so they can see her!"

"I really don't like the idea of you going on the ship all by yourself, Francis."

"I won't be by myself, Thomas. I'll be with Myra!" Francis laughed with excitement and mischief in her eyes.

"What about Emma and Dillyshane?"

"The Chinese houseboy takes care of them now. Why can't he be the one to take care of them while I'm gone?"

Thomas scowled. "And supper? Bedtime? What about then?"

"We can get Cheng to stay a bit longer to fix supper and get them ready for bed, I'm sure. Then, surely you can read a story and tuck them in, can't you, Thomas?" She was teasing him now and he knew it, but still it was hard for him to think of Francis alone on a ship.

"You know the answer to that one. It's just . . ." Thomas stopped.

"Just what?"

"You know what . . . I'll miss you! That's what!"

He stood up quickly and reached for Francis pulling her to her feet. His arms were around her and he was holding her close as he murmured again, and again, "I'll miss you, I'll miss you." She laid her head on Thomas's chest, knowing full well that he would miss her and that she would miss him, too.

"I know, Thomas. It's hard for us to be apart. But, it won't be for very long, I promise. Just long enough for my parents to see her while she's small like she is now."

Francis and little Myra left for Seattle by ship because it was the only way to get from San Francisco to Seattle. It was a lonely little family she left behind but she promised to be back soon. "Very soon," she smiled as she hugged Emma and Dillyshane. She lingered in Thomas's arms, reluctantly taking baby Myra from Cheng as the loud blast from the horn blew for non-passengers to exit the ship. Her little family on the landing for a long time, watching the ship pull away from the wharf and leave the harbor.

"When Mama come back?" Dillyshane wanted to know.

"In just a few weeks," Thomas replied as he hoisted his son up on his shoulder. "Come on, Cheng . . . Emma. We need to catch the next streetcar to take us back home."

Thomas, again at the wharf, agreed with Emma and Dillshane while they waited for the rest of their family to arrive from Seattle. It had been a very long six weeks that Francis and Myra were gone. Emma and Dillyshane waved frantically and shouted as soon as they spotted their mother carrying Myra and standing against the railing of the ship while it docked. Francis debarked among the very first of the people getting off the ship. She was coughing as she handed Myra to Thomas the minute she got close to him. She turned away from Emma and Dillyshane.

"Don't come near me, children! I have a very, very bad cold and I don't want you to get it from me! Oh, but it's wonderful to see you! Emma, you look marvelous . . . so grown up! And Dilly! You must be at least six inches taller than before I left!" She turned to Thomas. "I'm so sorry, Thomas, to bring this awful cold and cough home with me. Definitely not the gift I would have chosen."

"We are glad to see you, no matter what, Francis." Thomas wrapped his other arm around her and pulled her close to kiss her cheek. "Let's get us all home, shall we?"

This time Thomas spared no expense and hired a carriage to take Francis, her luggage, the three children and himself back home. They all talked a mile a minute on the way . . . the children full of questions about Seattle and their Lacey grandparents, then telling their mother stories about what had happened since she was away. There was much laughter and great happiness spoiled only by Francis's coughing. Thomas was worried about her and sent Cheng for the doctor the minute they arrived home. The doctor, however, couldn't come until the next morning.

After examining Francis he said, "I'm afraid you have more than a little cough, Francis. This is pneumonia you have, well advanced, too. I'll do my best for you. You must stay in bed and rest. The children should keep their distance. I'm leaving some cough medicine and these little white pills. I'll leave the pills and the instructions with Cheng. I think he'll be better at remembering the time and getting them to you. Drink plenty of water."

In spite of the cough medicine Francis coughed a great deal all during the night and became feverish. The doctor was summoned again. This time he shook his head as he talked with Thomas. "There's nothing else I can do, Thomas. We just have to pray that the medicine we're giving her will help. Stay with her all night tonight. I'll come by first thing in the morning."

Thomas was at Francis's bedside all night, spooning the cough medicine into her mouth, administering the little white pills, and carefully rubbing Watkins camphorated ointment on her neck and chest to help her breathe easier.

But still she coughed.

"Forgive me, Thomas," she whispered between coughing spells.

"I didn't think I was bringing this home to all of you. There was water on the cabin floor of the ship . . . my feet got wet."

"I know, dear. It's all right. Just don't try to talk. Rest. It's the best medicine. I'm right here with you, Francis. You are my love. I will never leave you."

Francis smiled wanly and pressed Thomas's hand to her cheek. She finally fell asleep as Thomas gently rubbed her arm and crooned softly to her.

But when the doctor came the next morning he was disappointed. Francis didn't show any improvement and her fever was still high. "You'll have to get a nurse, Thomas. She needs to be bathed to lower her fever, but she must not get chilled either. It's hard for you to be able to do that. I'll find someone to come."

The nurse came and immediately excluded all of the family from the sick room. It was hard for Thomas to be thrust aside from Francis, but he stayed close to the door of their room. Toward evening he persuaded the nurse to go downstairs for supper while he spent those spare moments with Francis. He was exhausted from being up all night the night before and when Nurse came back she sent him to bed saying she would call him if needed.

The very next morning Nurse called the family together, telling them that their mother wanted to see them all. Thomas carried little Myra and Cheng brought Emma and Dillyshane. Thomas was alarmed at how Francis looked. She seemed to have changed a great deal since the night before. He tried to put up a brave front for the children as they all took turns climbing up on the bed to be hugged by their mother. Emma was the only one who seemed to understand how dreadfully ill their mother was. She clung to her mother's hands until Thomas gently drew her away by telling her that her mother needed to rest.

After the children's visit Francis seemed to become weaker and Thomas felt she was giving up.

"Francis . . . I love you . . . we all love you . . . we need you. Don't give up, please, Francis, I beg you . . . please." This time the nurse didn't chase Thomas away. She herself went away from the sick room and waited downstairs with the children while Thomas and Francis spent this time together. Thomas held Francis in his arms until he could feel her weakened body give way and she became limp. Even then it was hard for him to release her and lay her body back on the bed.

The next hard thing for him was to tell the children.

Chapter Seven

$\mathcal{T}$he death of her mother had a profound effect on Emma. Overnight, she grew up. At nine years old she was soon directing Dillyshane, singing to baby Myra when she cried, and consulting with Cheng about meals and keeping the house clean.

Thomas watched Emma in amazement.

"Your mother would be so proud of you, Emma! I'm proud of you! What in the world would I do without you?" He hugged her and kissed the top of her head. Emma looked embarrassed but later Thomas noticed her smiling to herself and humming as she walked about the house.

One day Thomas sat down to consult with Emma. He held her hands as she stood in front of him.

"What would you think of our moving up to Seattle and being close to your Lacey grandparents?"

Emma's eyes lit up with pleasure at the thought. "I think that's a wonderful idea, Papa!" Then, as an afterthought, "Can we take Cheng with us? I don't know how we could get along without Cheng."

"I'm afraid that wouldn't be possible, Emma. Cheng has a family of his own that he needs to think of. He couldn't just leave them and go with us."

"Oh dear."

Thomas needed to think of his family too and felt he needed the help of the Lacey grandparents in raising the three children . . . even though Emma and Cheng were doing an excellent job. He needed new territory for selling encyclopedias and the return from lawyer work alone was not enough.

Cheng helped them pack and waved sadly as the family called their goodbyes to him from the carriage.

The children were excited about going on the ship.

"It's like the ship Mama went on, Dilly. Isn't this exciting?" Emma enjoyed taking Dillyshane around the ship exploring all the nooks and crannies, climbing the steps and learning some of the "ship language" of deck . . . gangway . . . stern . . . aft . . . bow . . . port . . . starboard . . . portholes. The list seemed endless as they consulted the crew and explored. Thomas was kept busy with little Myra and didn't get about the ship much, even though he walked the deck carrying Myra in his arms a few times each day. Dillyshane was beginning to show his resentment of his baby sister . . . silently, but it showed in his ignoring of her whenever all of them were together. He never played with her or even paid any attention to her at all. Thomas sensed this and never pressed the care or watching of Myra onto Dillyshane.

The children were excited to be going to see their grandparents and Thomas was both needing and looking forward to the Lacey's help. When they arrived in Seattle, both he and the children could not believe the huge change in the attitude of his wife's parents.

The Lacey's refused to help with the children.

Very soon after the Clarkes' moved to Seattle the Laceys packed up again and moved on, not even leaving Thomas with any information as to when or where they were going. Thomas was puzzled as they had always been caring and affectionate toward him and Francis and their young family. They had also relied on him to sell any property they purchased each time they moved on. This time they left the property they had acquired with someone else to sell.

Although Thomas was sadly disappointed with his in-laws, he was determined to stay on in Seattle and raise his children there. He bought a three-story house in Tacoma. He and the children lived on the main floor and he rented out the second and third floors to help pay the mortgage. He soon learned of a furniture store, also in Tacoma, that was for sale by an old man who wanted to get out of the business. He checked it out and wound up working out an arrangement of time payments to the old man hoping the store would supplement his income from lawyer work and the selling of encyclopedias.

Because there was now no help from grandparents and no Cheng with them, it was Emma who looked after Dillyshane and Myra, and did everything else. Thomas felt that Emma shouldn't have to do it alone, even though he was constantly amazed at how well she was able to cope. But she's only a child, he thought. I've got to find some help for her. Because Cheng had worked out well in San Francisco he put an ad in their local paper for another Chinese houseboy in Seattle.

Hui answered Thomas's ad by appearing on his doorstep in the morning the very next day.

"You need help, sir?" Hui bowed.

"Well . . . yes. Yes, I do. How did you know?"

"You put ad in paper, sir."

"But . . . the paper hasn't come out yet. Where did you see the ad?" he asked.

"I work . . . deliver paper."

"Then you already have a job . . ."

"Not my like job." Hui bowed again.

"Well . . . I guess you'd better come in so that we can talk." Thomas opened the door and motioned for Hui to enter. Hui came through the door, bobbing with his bows all the way.

"The first thing, Hui, is this . . . if I give you this job I don't want to see all this constant bowing all the time. Do you understand?"

Hui started to bow, then smiled at Thomas, stood up straight and said, "Yes, sir! Understand."

The result of the interview was Thomas hiring Hui. He learned Hui had a fair-sized family of five children at home but that he could still come daily to help Thomas and his little family of three.

Hui's first morning resulted in meeting Emma, who immediately took charge of telling Hui what was expected of him in the way of help.

"You will bath Myra, the baby, every morning, Hui," she began.

"Baby is girl name My-ra?"

"Yes. Then, there is my little brother who is named Dillyshane. He needs bathing, too, as he gets very dirty playing outside. Bathing him at night before we have supper works best."

"Dilly . . . ?"

"Dillyshane."

"Dilly . . . sha-a-ne."

"Yes, you said it right," Emma encouraged him.

"We will need to go to the market every morning. We take Myra and Dillyshane with us. You will keep track of them and help me by telling me what you will need to cook for us. I will do the shopping," she said firmly. She smiled, though, and Hui returned her smile, starting to again bow, but stopped and stood up straight.

"We go today?" he asked.

"Yes, today. I will be ready in fifteen minutes. You must get the children ready while I change my dress." Emma turned on her heel and walked away.

Emma smiled to herself, thinking there was no way Hui would be able to do it in fifteen minutes, but it was her own way of testing him for the job. She was definitely surprised, even on the verge of astonished when she went to the entryway after the designated fifteen minutes, to see Hui standing in the doorway with Myra in his arms and holding Dillyshane by the hand.

Emma smiled at Hui. "Shall we go?" she asked.

He had passed her entrance exam.

After Hui had been working for the Clarkes for a few weeks Thomas searched him out one day to question him.

"How are things working out, Hui? Are you getting along with the children?"

Hui stood up straight as he'd been told even though his inclination was to bow. "Yes. We do fine . . . little miss and me. She know best."

Thomas smiled. "Little miss is quite the person in charge, I'm afraid."

"Yes. She in charge. She know best."

"How about Dillyshane and the baby?"

"Dilly-sha-ane busy boy."

Thomas nodded. "And the baby?"

"Sweet baby. She good. She play."

"Are you happy here, Hui?"

This time Hui bowed and smiled, "Happy, sir. Ve-h-h-ry happy."

"Good. That's what I wanted to hear." Thomas sighed with relief. "I guess we're going to make it."

"We make it, sir. We make it good."

They did. Life became normal after Hui settled in with the family. Emma started going to school. Dillyshane was lonesome at first without Emma, but he soon became used to playing alone. The next two years flew by for Dillyshane in spite of his missing Emma. He was soon joining her at school and then the years flew even faster. The one he missed immensely was his mother. He never accepted the fact that she had come back from Seattle and died. Just like that. Gone forever. It changed him as he loved her dearly. He put the blame on Myra. If it hadn't been for her his mother would not have gone on that ship to Seattle. He never forgave his little sister. He left home, even before finishing school, wandering aimlessly, still harboring the resentment of his younger sister.

The school years for Emma and Dillyshane, and later Myra, went by exceedingly fast. It didn't seem possible it was time for Emma to go to a university, but it was and she went with Thomas's blessing. Two years at the University of Washington would fill the requirements for her to become a teacher.

She continued living in Seattle with Thomas and Myra while going to the University.

Emma Clarke - Graduate

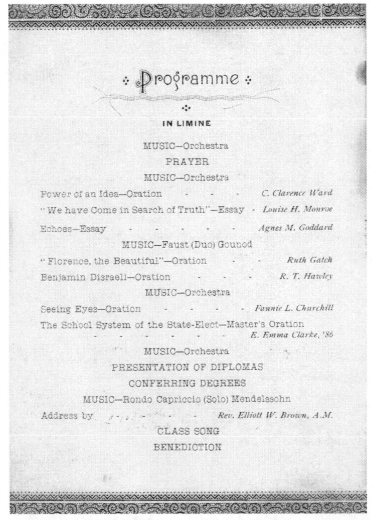

✦ Programme ✦

❖

IN LIMINE

MUSIC—Orchestra

PRAYER

MUSIC—Orchestra

Power of an Idea—Oration   -   -   -   *C. Clarence Ward*

"We have Come in Search of Truth"—Essay - *Louise H. Monroe*

Echoes—Essay   -   -   -   -   *Agnes M. Goddard*

MUSIC—Faust (Duo) Gounod

"Florence, the Beautiful"—Oration   -   -   *Ruth Gatch*

Benjamin Disraeli—Oration   -   -   -   *R. T. Hawley*

MUSIC—Orchestra

Seeing Eyes—Oration   -   -   -   -   *Fannie L. Churchill*

The School System of the State-Elect—Master's Oration
   -   -   -   -   -   -   *E. Emma Clarke, '86*

MUSIC—Orchestra

PRESENTATION OF DIPLOMAS

CONFERRING DEGREES

MUSIC—Rondo Capriccio (Solo) Mendelssohn

Address by   -   -   -   -   *Rev. Elliott W. Brown, A.M.*

CLASS SONG

BENEDICTION

When Emma began thinking about a teaching job the best offer seemed to be one from the small town of Woodinville, north of Seattle itself. She would have to figure out just what to do about a place to live if she accepted that one. Woodinville was too far away from Thomas's home for her to travel back and forth every day.

Chapter Eight

*T*homas straightened the engineering equipment, lined up the reference books on the shelf and busied himself about his store. It was mid-morning when Hazen Pratt walked in the door . . . first customer of the day. It had been an unusually quiet beginning.

"Good morning, Sir!"

"Good morning. Thank you for the Sir," Hazen laughed, looking at his travel worn clothes and calloused hands.

"You look like a "Sir" to me, Sir!" Thomas replied, joining Hazen in laughing. "What can I do for you today?"

"I'm Hazen Pratt," the new customer said as he held out his hand.

Thomas grasped it and smiled, "Thomas Clarke . . . happy to have you in the store. Have you been traveling far to get here?"

"Yes, indeed! I rowed across the sound this morning. It was a little further than I thought it was going to be. Good exercise though." Hazen looked around the store, rubbing his hands together until he spotted some equipment he was going to need within the next month of surveying. As he looked about he carried on a conversation with Thomas. The two chatted easily and found they had much in common. Time flew by while Hazen checked for his supplies and Thomas waited on other customers who came in during the afternoon. Thomas soon realized there was not going to be enough time for Hazen to row back across the sound before dark.

The two were already on a first name basis, giving Thomas the familiarity with which to say, "Hazen, you won't have time to make it back across the pond before nightfall. Come home with me for supper. We've got a cot on the sleeping porch where you can sleep the night, too."

Hazen looked outside, then at the clock on the wall.

"I guess we lost track of time, didn't we? It's really good of you to ask me for supper . . . and a place to sleep, too."

"Think nothing of it, my friend." Thomas looked at the clock himself then and said, "Looks like it's time to close up the store."

He pulled shades down on the big store windows, took a key off the hook near the front door and found his hat.

Thomas Dowling Clarke as an older man.

A young George Hazen Pratt

The two men were of a height . . . both tall and slender with dark hair. Thomas admired his newfound friend and thought him handsome as well as easy to talk with. They had become friends more quickly than he could have imagined.

When they reached Thomas's home, as he was about to open the front door he said, "My daughters live with me here. The younger one isn't home this week, but Emma should be here. She's going to the University. We'll see."

Emma was home. She came running toward the front door wiping her hands on her apron and smiling, "Oh, I thought I had locked the door and I was coming to let you in, Papa." She kissed him on the cheek before she was aware that Thomas was not alone.

"Emma, this is Hazen Pratt. I've invited him for supper. I hope there will be enough."

"Oh yes, Papa. I'm sure there is enough." She turned to Hazen. "How do you do, Mr. Pratt . . . welcome." Emma smiled, nodding toward Hazen, her bright blue eyes sparkling at him.

He was immediately impressed and very nearly overwhelmed but managed to get his first words out, "How do you do, Miss Clarke."

"If you'll excuse me, I'll finish preparations for supper." Emma turned around and went back into the kitchen.

The men washed up, Hazen combing his hair and brushing at his clothes, in an attempt to look more presentable. They sat chatting in the living room until Emma came to call them to eat.

"If you would sit here, Mr. Pratt," Emma said, gesturing to a chair on the side of the dining room table. Her father was about to sit at the head. Hazen couldn't help but notice the slim figure of Emma as she directed him and sat down opposite her father.

Supper progressed with more conversation between Thomas and Hazen, with Emma speaking only in reference to the serving and passing of the food. She listened carefully to the men, wanting to join in the talk but remained quiet, still a bit hesitant to speak up.

As they rose from the table after consuming Emma's special chocolate cake for dessert, Thomas said to Emma, "I've invited Hazen to spend the night . . . told him he could sleep on the cot on the sleeping porch, Emma. Can you find a blanket and a pillow for him?"

"Yes, of course, Papa."

She began clearing the table and carrying things to the kitchen. The next thing she knew Hazen was gathering the serving bowls from the table.

"I think this young lady could use some help, he explained to his host as he carried bowls and platter to the kitchen.

Thomas went back to his office and sat down at his desk to do some calculations and ordering of supplies.

Emma was embarrassed to have Hazen coming into her kitchen.

"You don't have to do this, Mr. Pratt. I can manage."

"I believe your father said you were a student at the University. Surely you have some studies you should be doing this evening?"

"We-l-l-l-l, yes, I do, but guests shouldn't have to carry dishes."

"Never mind that. Your father has some work to do in his office and I would be more than happy to help you wash up these dishes."

Hazen continued to clear the table and bring things to the kitchen while Emma put the leftover food away and filled the dishpan with hot water and soap. Hazen found the towels and began rinsing and drying the dishes. He gave up on calling Emma "Miss Clarke" as it sounded altogether too formal for this lovely, friendly young woman.

"Tell me, Emma, what are you studying . . . what is your main idea for going to the University?"

"I want to teach school. In fact, there is a place waiting for me to teach as soon as I finish at the University."

"Really? How did that come about?" he asked.

"They published a list at school, a list of places that need teachers. I answered a few and one place wrote back that they had had several applications but mine appealed to them the most and they would like to hire me. I start teaching there in September."

"That sounds very good indeed. Where is it?" Hazen asked as he hung up the towel and leaned back against the sink edge looking at Emma. He was enjoying this attractive young woman.

"Woodinville, Washington."

"Woodinville, Washington. I know where that is. I surveyed that area about five years ago."

"And where are you surveying now, Mr. Pratt?"

"I'm heading out on a new job next week surveying the Yukon."

"The Yukon is a good distance north of Washington . . . almost to the Artic Circle," Emma said.

"Well, actually the northernmost part of the Yukon is within the Artic Circle."

"That makes it sound far, far away." Emma said wistfully.

"It is pretty far. I don't think I'll be dropping in to have supper with you from there!"

Emma smiled.

"It will be lonesome, won't it, Mr. Pratt?"

"Yes, I expect it will. The only contact we'll have will be the mail which we will receive every three weeks or so, I understand."

"That certainly isn't very often. You must look forward to those mail deliveries."

"It would give me something extra special to look forward to if you wrote to me, Emma."

"Then I shall write you, Mr. Pratt. You will have to write me first, however, so I know the address."

"I will do that, Emma."

Just then Thomas came to the kitchen door inquiring, "What will you do, Hazen? Has my daughter talked you into something?"

"I think perhaps I've talked her into something. She has promised to write me while I'm surveying the Yukon, so I just told her I would send her my address as soon as I know what it is."

"Letters will be most welcome there, I can imagine."

"Yes, sir, they most certainly will."

Emma left the two men saying their goodnights while she rounded up blankets and a pillow for the cot on the sleeping porch. When she returned she said, "I hope these will be enough to keep you warm, Mr. Pratt. It gets quite cool out here during the night."

"You don't need to worry on that account. I sleep outside all the time when I am out on a surveying assignment. I'm used to it. In fact, I feel smothered when put inside a closed room to sleep."

"I'm so glad we have a sleeping porch for you then, Mr. Pratt." Emma smiled and turned to leave.

"Emma, just a minute," Hazen stopped her. "I've been thinking since we talked about your job offer in Woodinville. I know a number of people that live there and I can refer you to someone that could help you find a place to live . . . in fact, you might even be able to stay with them if they have no roomers just now."

Emma's eyes lit up. "Oh, could you? How very thoughtful of you, Mr. Pratt." She smiled shyly looking up at him. "Perhaps you could write the names down for me in the morning."

"Yes, I will. In fact, if you can supply me with the paper, I have a pen and can start making a list tonight."

"Of course, Mr. Pratt."

She turned to leave the porch with Hazen not taking his eyes off her. He admired everything about her . . . her posture, her walk, her slim figure, her dark shining hair, her smile and those blue, blue eyes. When she returned with paper for him it was all he could do to keep from gathering her up in his arms.

"Good night, Mr. Pratt."

"Good night, Emma," he smiled at her, watching her as she left the room.

Whatever is the matter with me, he thought. I've never felt like this in my life before. I'm having all I can do to keep from putting my arms around her. Haze, old boy, you'd better watch it.

In the morning Emma was up early, had prepared breakfast for Thomas and Hazen and now was at the front door with books in her arms, ready to depart for school as Hazen came into the living room.

"Well! You're an early bird," Hazen smiled, walking toward her. He was holding the paper she'd given him the night before. "I've made the list of people I know in Woodinville. I hope it will be helpful."

"Oh, I'm sure it will be. You are so kind to do that. Thank you, Mr. Pratt. I'm sorry to hurry away but I have class in twenty minutes."

"Quite all right. I hope to see you again before I leave for the Yukon," Hazen said, hopefully.

"I'm sure we will see you again. Papa won't let that happen without you coming by to see us before you leave. Bye-bye for now, Mr. Pratt."

Hazen had walked to the door. "Let me get the door for you. You have your arms full." He tucked the list of Woodinville people under the flap of the top book in her arms before opening the door.

"Thank you, Mr. Pratt."

He heaved a big sigh as he closed the door after Emma. "She even smells heavenly."

"What's that, Hazen?" Thomas asked as he came into the room. "Did Emma leave without breakfast for us this morning?"

"I really couldn't say, sir. I didn't ask and she didn't tell me."

"I guess we will just have to look in the kitchen, then." Thomas headed for the kitchen . . . calling out to Hazen. "Breakfast is all set out here for us, Hazen. She is some fine daughter, wouldn't you say?"

"Yes, sir. She most definitely is a very fine daughter." Hazen smiled.

As it turned out, Hazen and Emma didn't have another chance to talk. All the things he needed for his surveying trip into the Yukon were on hand in Thomas's store. Hazen purchased everything, tied it all up carefully and carried it down to the rowboat he had anchored at the shore. There was no need to stay over another night. Thomas was unusually busy at the store so Hazen decided to just shove off and start the long row back across the sound.

For someone who usually felt an inner peace and general happiness with life, this morning Hazen felt cheated and disappointed. He had so much hoped to see Emma again before he took off into the unknown once more.

"I'll just have to write to her right away," he mumbled to himself as he rowed steadily. "I don't have her address, but I can send it to the store," he turned and checked behind himself to see that his direction was correct. All was good. "Thomas will see that she gets it, I'm sure." There was more rowing with more talking. "What a delightful person that girl is . . . never met anyone like her before . . . wonder how she feels about me . . . just have to wait and see . . . so pretty . . . never knew anyone with such blue eyes . . . and her smile . . . what a wonderful smile she has. Guess I'm a goner. I wonder how old she is . . . still at the University . . . must be about twenty . . . maybe she'll think I'm too old for her . . . maybe age doesn't matter to her . . . oh, give it up, Hazen."

The rest of the way across the sound he rowed steady, but was quiet. No more conjecturing to himself. Time alone would tell was the thought that kept running through his mind.

Chapter Nine

$\mathcal{T}$homas was concerned with his younger daughter Myra as well as with Emma. He felt they needed a female to confide in and consult with, but what could he do? He had counted, more than he realized at the time, on the help of the Laceys. Now it seemed to be up to him, or the Chinese houseboy, or Emma to help Myra. Now that Emma was completely grown up and finishing her university training, he felt he could consult with her. She was more than twenty-one. She had become an adult.

Myra and Emma didn't share a room, which did nothing to foster any closeness between them. They actually led entirely separate lives from each other, both in school and social activities. One evening when Thomas let himself into the house after working the day at the store he realized Myra wasn't home. He cornered Emma in the kitchen.

"Emma, I need to talk to you."

"Papa, I'm fixing our supper!" Emma was obviously in the midst of a number of things going on in the kitchen.

"I know, dear, but I need to talk to you before Myra comes home."

"She's not coming home tonight, Papa. Can this wait 'til supper?"

"In that case, yes, it can wait 'til supper."

Thomas turned, head down, thoughtful, walking back into the living room to his favorite chair where he sat pondering just how to question Emma as well as how to deal with Myra.

It was hard for Thomas to not blurt out immediately his thoughts, but it didn't seem fair after Emma had worked so hard to prepare the food he saw before him. The two ate and chatted, each about their days. Finally, Thomas said, "Emma, I need to consult with you about Myra."

"Myra? What about Myra?"

"She has such big ideas," Thomas began.

"Big ideas are good, aren't they, Papa? I had big ideas and I wound up going to Washington University!"

"Yes, but Myra is talking about learning to teach Home Economics and the only place to get that sort of an education is back east in New York."

"Oh." Emma sat quietly for a bit before she dared look up at her father. "What does that mean for you, Papa?"

"I guess it means I would have to move to New York with her so she can attend that school."

Emma's eyes glistened.

"Oh, Papa, I would miss you so much."

"I know, dear, and I don't know how I could get along without you." He reached across the table and took Emma's hand.

Emma managed to not shed the tears in her eyes as she squeezed her father's hand. "You have to do what you think is best, Papa . . . when the time comes you will be able to make the best decision."

This time it was Thomas who was near tears.

Emma's last semester at the University was nearly over. Final examinations were coming up. She was deep into studying for them late one afternoon at home. She had put dinner in the oven earlier and was poring over her books when Thomas came home and was unlocking the front door.

"Anyone home?" he called as he opened the door and hung his coat up in the entry.

"I'm here, Papa. Getting ready for final exams." Emma got up and went to her father with a welcoming kiss on the cheek. "I put our supper in the oven so it should be ready about now."

She started toward the kitchen, stopped and turned saying, "Myra is staying over for supper with the Baxters, so it's just you and me, Papa."

"I'll not complain, Emma. By the way," he said as he started to wash up for supper, "There's a letter for you in my coat pocket in the hall. Forgot about it until I saw you. Fetch it will you?"

"Of course, Papa. But . . . a letter for me coming to the store?"

"Yes," Thomas called. "I think it's from that Hazen Pratt fellow."

Emma stopped. "That Hazen Pratt fellow." She thought he had forgotten. But he hadn't! She ran to the entry rummaging in her father's overcoat pockets to find the letter.

After they had eaten supper and the dishes were done, Emma, supposedly back to her studies, was instead writing a letter . . . in answer to the one from Hazen that she had found in her father's coat pocket. She spent more than an hour telling him about school, exams and the latest news from her family. She herself was surprised at the time she spent writing "Mr. Pratt" when she would ordinarily have been studying. She posted her letter the next morning on her way to school, having put her home address on the outside so that his answer might come there instead of to her father's store.

She kept watching for a return letter from "Mr. Pratt" and finally was happy to see a letter for her, but this time it was from Grandfather Clarke.

Pataskala, Ohio -
14th Septr. 1886

My dear Emma,
Your kind favor and Photos came safe and in nice order. I cannot tell you how proud I felt in having a granddaughter capable of achieving so grand a triumph as you have done, and hope it is a prelude to still greater achievements. The Photos are grand, I chose the standing figure, which looks the lady in every particular. Aunt Mary and Eliza took the others. We all think highly of them. We are glad to have one scholar in the family. I hope Myra and Dilly will follow your good example and try to be good scholars. Youth in the present day have greater facilities for learning than there were seventy-five years ago when I went to school. We had not the variety of Textbooks that are in use in the present day. We went to school in the morning at 7 o'clock, to breakfast at 9 o'clock, back at 10 and quit at 3 o'clock (Dinner) and on Saturday's we quit at noon. I have some of my old copies, a geography book, published in 1803 and edited by John Sherman . . . also, an Atlas which contains only a few of the States that were in this country at that day. There was more attention paid to good spelling than there is at present.

The last letter I received from your Pa was from Oregon. I enclose an answer to it, you can write his address on it and forward it. I wish he could get some good employment near his home. It must be a great privation to him to be separated from his family. We all wonder how you ever managed to keep through the ordeal of housekeeping, and pursue your studies. You are one girl in a hundred that could do so, and your father is highly favored in having so good a daughter.

All my folks join in love and best wishes to you, Myra and Dilly, and may God help and prosper you all, is the prayer of your affectionate grandpa_____

Edw. D. Clarke

The last sentence was added upside down on the top of the first page of Edward's letter to Emma. She smiled at this and was happy to have a letter from her grandfather, but still she kept hoping . . . and looking for . . . a letter from "Mr. Pratt."

Emma graduated from the University of Washington in June of 1886. Her graduation ceremonies were over before Hazen's next letter came for her. She opened it eagerly.

Snohomish, July 31st

My Dear Friend:

How am I going to confess that I was in Seattle last night? Just a few hours row from Tacoma. I hardly know how it was, but I made an unexpected trip into town rather than remain at West Coast Junction. (Strange, wasn't it?) And when I found myself there I decided that railroad business and making calls were incompatible, particularly as I came from camp, the resources of which are limited. My assignment to the Yukon seems to have been put off for a bit.

I trust that you are enjoying your vacation, as you are certainly entitled to do after a long term of school.

I have abandoned my camp and have moved here. I board at a private house. They allowed me to pitch my tent in the yard and I use it for an office as well as a place where tired nature seeks the sweet restorer. Old Dr. Towndrow, whom I have known for some time, boards here and today seemed much disappointed because I did not bring Mrs. P. back with me. He insists upon there being such a person in existence, and of course, I am too wise to dispute with him.

I shall be rather busy here until I finish my work on this Division, but will hope for an occasional day by myself.

I am wondering when I may hear from you.

Sincerely,
G. Hazen Pratt

Emma was indignant at Hazen's last words, "I am wondering when I may hear from you." I wrote him quite some time ago, she thought. She immediately sat down with pen in hand, writing her indignation with such pressure on her pen it nearly punctured the paper on which she was writing.

Thomas wandered into the room and looked inquiringly at his daughter.

"Are we having supper tonight, Emma?" he asked.

Emma jumped up quickly. "I'm sorry, Papa. I was writing to Mr. Pratt. He wondered if he might hear from me and I felt I must explain that I have already written to him . . . several weeks ago, in fact."

Emma said it so emphatically Thomas felt compelled to tell her why she might not have heard from Hazen before.

"Well, Emma . . . when a man moves about as much as Hazen does it may take awhile for a letter to catch up with him."

"Oh, dear. I should have remembered that." She picked up the paper she had been writing on, looked at it thoughtfully, then tore it into several pieces. "I will start over after supper, Papa. My scolding would not be welcomed by Mr. Pratt, I'm sure."

She hurried into the kitchen to begin putting their supper on the table.

Immediately after supper Emma was again at her writing table, pen in hand, writing to "Mr. Pratt," never dreaming it was to be the beginning of a long, prolific correspondence between the two of them.

The next day Emma began consulting her father about something else.

"Papa, I wonder what you would think if I decided to invest in some vacant land?"

"Land is always a good investment, Emma." Thomas smiled at his daughter. He was proud of her and her question now intensified his pride.

"I've heard of 'homesteading'."

"No money required for homesteading, I understand."

"Is there any reason why I couldn't do that?" Emma asked.

"The only problem then is that you have to live on the property you homestead for six months of the year."

"Yes, I know, Papa." Emma was thoughtful. "That means I would have to build something on it."

"Nelson could help you out on that, I'm sure, Emma."

"Oh, I had forgotten about Nelson. He could, couldn't he?" Emma was suddenly energized. She jumped up with a big smile and ran to hug her father.

This was a new avenue of thought and action for Emma. She was teaching every day, plus now she was searching for properties that could be homesteaded. When she found something she would begin consulting with their friend Nelson.

It wasn't many weeks before Emma filed the papers to homestead forty acres of vacant land she had located. She hired Nelson to build a small one-room cabin on the land and had a few basic necessities hauled up to furnish it. Now the problem was how to live in the cabin and still keep teaching school. It was entirely too far away to walk every day. She moved in during the summer, enjoying the lovely warm weather, exploring the area all around her cabin and continuing her correspondence with Hazen.

"Emma, how are you going to get to school from your cabin?" Thomas quizzed her once when she came by to see him. "That's quite a walk to make every single day in the cold weather coming up soon."

"I've been thinking about that, too, Papa. Guess what?" She grinned at him mischievously.

"What, dear girl? What?" Thomas grinned back at her.

"I'm going to buy a horse."

"You're going to buy a horse?"

"Yes, I'm going to buy a horse."

"After your residency time is up what will you do with the horse?"

"That is a problem, I admit, Papa."

"How about renting, or maybe borrowing a horse for those few months you'll have left?"

"Do you know where I could find a horse to rent or borrow, Papa?"

"This is another time when Nelson will come in handy. Why don't you ask him? He might let you use his horse or at least know of another one you could borrow for a short time."

"Oh, Papa, you are so good at helping me solve my problems!" She gave Thomas a hug and kissed his cheek.

Emma wound up borrowing Nelson's own horse and renting a sidesaddle so she could be wearing her dress ready for school when she left home each morning. It was only to be for a few short weeks.

As soon as Emma's six months residency was over she was once again living at home with Thomas, Dillyshane and Myra.

Chapter Ten

*H*azen's letters to Emma always began with the heading of his location. Because it was very often uncharted territory he then wrote the longitude and latitude along with the date and the number of his camp. It was difficult to be separated by many miles and time, but as the months and years went by they became accustomed to the separations. The letters from Hazen were cherished by Emma. She kept them all and tied them together with a red ribbon, undoing the ribbon many times to take out and reread Hazen's faithful letter writing. He made a trip back to his birthplace in Vermont in January of 1888 and wrote several letters back to his newfound love.

Beulah Farm, Vermont is the home
of the Pratt boys and Lizzie.

West Hartford, Jan. 6, 1888

My Dearest Emma____

Lizzie and I went to church today. Are you surprised at my going? Oh, you don't know whether I generally go or not. Wasn't it reckless of you to care so much for me without knowing me? Or did you think you knew me somewhat? I am constantly learning about you, my own, and you are completely unaware. Such perfectly sweet things I read about you in a letter I rec'd today. Can you imagine who wrote it?

It has been raining a little all day, freezing as it fell, but "Mollie"____ Arthur's horse ____ took us safely down the hills. You see, we live two miles from the village with the nearest neighbor half a mile away. That sounds lonely, but it isn't a bit.

We got "the mail," for there might be a letter from my love and there <u>was</u>, also one from Miss Vannie which was perfectly splendid. I read it to Lizzie, explaining here and there.

She told me among other things that you were the dearest girl in the land. That was nothing new to me for I found it out some time ago.

She also told me to hurry back for "Emma's countenance lengthened visibly when she read that you intended to remain at Edge Moor for a while."

My dearest one, it is because I love you so, that I will go back there. You did not murmur ____ only told me of the "peculiar sensation in your throat" at what you felt might be a disappointment. If I did not care for you with my whole heart I am sure I should, knowing that you trust me so perfectly, and sometime soon, beloved, I will certainly come.

Many thanks for the newspapers. They look very familiar. The pen wiper is a perfect treasure. I will keep it by me constantly. I do not need it to remember you because since you sent the likeness of your dear face I have seen it oftener than every day.

Won't you please take a school near there and let someone else take charge of those boys? I will come every Saturday afternoon if you'll let me. I wish Edge Moor was at Kirkland.

Today is another raining day. It is regular Puget Sound winter weather.

Lizzie sends her love. (You see I've confided in her.) And I send more than one train can carry.

Thine own Hazen

Emma, when is your birthday? Did you ever tell me? If not, I beg your forgiveness for not asking you before. Hazen

Emma decided that it was time she moved out of her father's home and became more independent. Thomas was sorry to see her leave the rest of the family but he understood and was more proud of her than he admitted to anyone. She moved into a boarding house operated by a Mrs. Greene who kept a close watch on "her girls." When school started again in September Emma began teaching on Vashon Island in Puget Sound in the Washington Territory. She had seventeen pupils and taught in a newly constructed building amidst a forest of trees. Getting there required her to take a ferryboat from the mainland. She loved it all . . . the freshness of the breeze off the water, the forest, even the children in whom she hoped to smooth out the roughness and instill a love and pride of learning.

Hazen was at last back in Washington when Emma began receiving his notes from closer by again. He came into Seattle to visit her and met her roommates at Mrs. Greene's boarding house.

Snohomish, Sept. 11, 1888

My Dear Emma,

Your kind letter reached me tonight just as I thought it would for steamboat transportation is not the most rapid in the world. No, I was not sure it would come tonight, for I was disappointed when I failed to get it last night for I knew it was on the road. What a delightful place you have there with your friends! I don't mind your telling them so, for I simply fell in love with their charming ways, and I will not forget the pleasure it gave me to know them. Of course it is because I am your friend but it is so much the more to be appreciated on that account.

I am very sorry that I didn't see Miss Greene. Doubtless my sorrow is one of my punishments for wrong-doing.

I reached "Guiteau's" tent about eight, Sunday night, and he kindly arranged for me to stay with him. The next morning the train brought me over to Snohomish and here I have found work enough to keep me tolerably busy since. I think I shall remain here the greater part of this month, and then no one knows whither.

Eight days later, Hazen wrote again. Emma was very interested in his thoughts concerning *the letter from Baker Moore about which she had written him.*

I would suggest that your letter from Baker Moore & Co. was simply a means of procuring your address and that probably you will receive information to the effect that they are "searchers of records," etc., etc. perhaps on account of your having filed under a piece of land lately...
The first passenger train crossed the Snohomish Bridge today. Some ladies decorated the engine with flowers, and gave the engineer a nice bouquet.
I will try and be at Juanita on Sunday. I expect Mr. Holbrook on Saturday, so I do not dare to make any plans for that day, but hoping to have the pleasure of seeing Juanita (and hearing it) soon. I must close. My best love, Hazen

Two days later Hazen writes once more.

It will be impossible for me to go to Juanita this week. The San Francisco Bridge Co. is about to finish their work here and it is necessary for me to look after all details of the work before they leave it. They will work on Sunday, hence the necessity of my being here. I regret it very much. Hastily, Hazen

In October of 1888 Emma had an interesting communication from Hazen. She was much relieved after reading it knowing how unhappy Hazen had been.

Snohomish, Oct. 1st, 1888

My Dearest Emma,

I found the construction train at West Coast Junction and was in Snohomish at 12 o'clock. So, you see, I am quite glad that I remained at Mr. Hawley's Saturday night.

Yes, I am going to ask to be relieved at once . . . something I should have done long ago. I must remember to refer to him properly. The man with many initials who keeps watch of this part of the work . . . West Coast . . . is simply unbearable. I haven't felt so well for months as I have since I came to this conclusion. Mr. Stixrud approves, and thought I ought to have done so last week. He . . . Stixrud . . . has been ordered to Spokane and goes to Seattle with me.

With much love . . . Hazen

Emma wrote many letters besides the ones to "Mr. Pratt." She carried on a correspondence through the years with her grandfather Edward Dowling Clarke, who still resided in Pataskala, Ohio.

Pataskala, O. 28th December 1886

My dear Emma,

Last evening I received a letter from your Pa, dated the 24th, sent from Kansas City, Mo. in which he requested me to send you $20. This I now do, in the shape of a postal order payable to you at Seattle and which I herewith enclose. I presume your Pa will write you how he wishes it applied.

I hope to hear that you are all well. Aunt Mary and her family took dinner with us on Christmas Day; we spoke of our absent friends, and regretted our being so scattered as to prevent our enjoying a happy reunion.

Eliza and Lottie sent you some Photos lately and which they hope reached you safely.

Now, Emma, as you are the oldest, I trust you will do what you can to cheer up your dear Pa. He sounded so tired and discouraged in his letter.

Grandma Clarke and Eliza write in love to you all. Wishing you many happy New Years, I remain as ever,

Your affectionate grand-pa
Edw. D. Clarke

Thomas had been called to Kansas City to take care of business related to part of the Francis Lacey Clarke's family living there and he was discouraged with being so far from his family. He worried about his store as he had just locked the door and walked away when he was called to Kansas.

Thomas's bachelor brother Jacob was a driver for the Wells Fargo Stagecoach line and out on the road most of the time, but he came back to brother Thomas's home to check on the children weekends which was more than Thomas himself could do while he was out selling his American Biography Encyclopedia, doing his legal work, plus running a store. He was happy indeed to have things change for him during the following year. He was again back in Tacoma with Emma, Dillyshane and Myra. A greatly relieved Hiu was happy to have him back home. He had been concerned when he had to leave the little family alone each night.

Once again Thomas had relied on his brother and both Emma and Hiu. They hadn't let him down.

Pataskala, Ohio-

Monday, 10th October 1887.

My dear Son,

Your kind favor of last month and its enclosure reached me safely. For the latter accept my sincere thanks. Circumstanced as you are I had no expectancy of your being so liberal towards me, and therefore I appreciate your gift the more. May God help and prosper you, and spare you to your dear children whom I sincerely hope and trust will become good and useful members in society, and in your old age extend to you the same helping hand that you have done so kindly to me.

Emma wrote me of your store in the city, I am glad to hear about it, and hope it will soon be profitable. It will be so pleasant now to be back with your children.

Well, I have passed the eighty seventh (87) mile-stone in my life's journey in health, peace and safety, and feel grateful to my Heavenly Father for his sparing mercy. I have fully recovered from the severe illness I had last spring, and I feel that "Richard's himself again." I presume you and your folks are well, as you make no mention of them. Mother and Eliza are well.

I will send you some papers with an account of Mr. Cleveland's movements. This being President reminds me of a story told of an Irishman who was a short time here and wrote to his brother in Ireland...... "Dear Pat, Come out here soon as you can. Mighty MEAN men get into office here."

When I left Ireland I did so with regret. Now, I thank God that I am here. Poor, unfortunate priest-ridden Ireland is made a subject for every political anatomist to exercise his talents upon. It appears to me that a crisis is coming, when both this country and Europe and other nations will be involved in a general overthrow. I don't expect to be living to see it. All with me join in love to you and the children.

Ever your affectionate father,
Edw. D. Clarke

Emma kept very busy with her teaching job and a social life soon established with the other female boarders at Mrs. Greene's. She continued her avid correspondence with Hazen. Now he was writing from Vermont where he had been called to help his sister Lizzie care for their brother Arthur who was quite ill. The correspondence between Hazen and Emma became more and more intimate, the salutations and closings of his letters showing how he felt about her.

It surprised Emma when she realized how happy she was to have Hazen back in Washington. At least his headquarters were in Washington, although sometimes his work took him quite a distance from Tacoma and Vashon Island. She often had short notes from him telling her when he would be nearby and hoped to see her. She found it difficult to conceal her delight in seeing him each time.

"Oh, Emma, I am so happy to see you!" Hazen took her hands in his but was still hesitant to draw her into his arms until he could tell just how she felt about him.

She clung to his hands and those blue, blue eyes glowed as she looked up at him. "As I am to see you, Mr. Pratt," she always said but would turn away before he could bend closer. Finally one evening when Hazen showed up at Mrs. Greenes' boarding house to see Emma she decided she must stop pulling away from this wonderful person who persisted quietly in coming to see her.

"Hello, Emma." Hazen smiled, reaching for her hands as soon as she came into Mrs. Greene's 'receiving room.'

"Mr. Pratt." She clung to his hands and raised her face to him, smiling directly into his eyes. As he bent to her his arms automatically found their way around her, drawing her closer to him, and as she didn't turn away he kissed her softly on her mouth. "Oh, Mr. Pratt . . . " She was trembling but took comfort in Hazen's arms. "Are you sure . . . ? "

"I've never been more sure of anything in my life, dear Emma. I've wanted to do this ever since I first laid eyes on you."

Emma leaned into Hazen, her head on his chest.

"I must have been wanting you to, Mr. Pratt, because it feels so right for me to be in your arms." They stood together, each comforted by the other. Fortunately, no one else was in Mrs. Greene's receiving room and they could hold each other for as long as they chose. Finally Hazen drew Emma over to the sofa in the room and they sat down together still holding hands.

"I do love you so, Emma. This is much better than writing about how much I love you in a letter. I've hesitated as I didn't know how you felt about me."

"I've been extremely flattered by your letters and your attention, Mr. Pratt, but I haven't dared to admit, even to myself, how I felt about you." Emma drew back and looked at Hazen. "I do dare now, however." She smiled at Hazen her blue eyes dancing.

"And?" Hazen asked anxiously.

"I find that I care very much for you. And . . . tonight I know for sure how much I care." She had stopped teasing him.

Hazen gathered her in his arms again, holding her close and whispering into her soft dark hair.

"I'm so glad."

They stayed, wrapped in each other's arms for quite some time and no doubt would have stayed longer if another boarder at Mrs. Greene's had not come into the room. They drew apart immediately.

"Ah, Miss Clarke! I was sent to find you and call you in to supper."

"Thank you, Mr. Jackson. Tell Mrs. Greene that I shall be right there." She turned to Hazen. "Shall I ask permission for you to join us at the supper table, Mr. Pratt?"

"I will only say yes because it allows me to be close to you and look at you and perhaps touch your hand now and then," Hazen said.

Emma smiled and they rose together. "Excuse me just for a moment," she said.

While she was gone Hazen stood, brushed at his hair and straightened his jacket, searching for a mirror. There was no mirror in sight so he just remained standing . . . waiting quietly for Emma.

When she returned the two went together into Mrs. Greene's dining room to enjoy eating supper together with the other boarders. Hazen did touch Emma's hand surreptitiously under the table and she was only too willing to let him hold it.

"I'm so happy you could join us for supper, Mr. Pratt." Emma smiled at Hazen, her blue eyes sparkling at him as they always did.

Chapter Eleven

*T*he number of Hazen's letters to Emma intensified as their relationship became more intimate.

Washington Camp, Nov. 5, 1889

My darling Emma,

Two letters came Saturday night and one last night. The first mentioned have been in Snohomish for about ten days while I have been all that time disconsolate. I see that you were very good and wrote when you were being neglected ____ sweet child ____ I will send you a kiss. But it was very good of you.

It will be impossible for me to be in Seattle Saturday ____ how sorry I am, love, but I cannot.

You will have a pleasant visit and I will try to go to Tacoma a week later. There is no train leaving Snohomish at 1:30 p.m. on Saturday so I will leave early in the morning and probably arrive in Tacoma late in the afternoon, returning early enough to take the Sunday p.m. train for Snohomish. I seem to be planning on a certainty but unfortunately it is not ____ but still I see no reason now why I cannot go. At the present time the work is somewhat behind on account of a location poorly done. I mean by this that the work of running the lines was poorly done, for some of the tangents are far from being straight and the curves have elbows in them sharp as an old maids. We intend to move camp farther up the line to a more convenient place for I find ten miles a day rather more than I care to undertake. At this time we are working until late every evening, but hope to have enough accomplished within a week so that it will not crowd us so badly.

I finished "Middlemarch" one day in a stagecoach riding from a little town called Harrisburg to Columbus. I remember less about the story than I do about the dusty road. That was one summer day in 1883 and I was not so much as dreaming about Washington, the great state of the Northwest, or the sweet girl that I was to find there.

I hope Mrs. Lee's cough has disappeared. Please give them my kindest regards when you have time.

Lovingly,
Hazen

Wash'n, Engineer's Camp, Nov. 13, 1889

My Dearest Emma:

We are at last moved, that is, partially. The team made only one trip today and as the distance is something less than four miles you can imagine the state of the roads. Office tent and the men's tent are here and pitched, but the kitchen and cook will not arrive until tomorrow. We would be in a sad plight were it not for the contractor's camp near by. It is quite cool tonight and the stoves are left behind. Mr. Stixrud showed his inventive genius by making one, which consists of an old tin bucket turned upside down, then a powder can on that with a hole cut in the side near the bottom for draught, and another in the top for the pipe to go over. The wood has to be made very small and when it needs firing up the pipe is moved to one side and wood put in at the place where the smoke escapes. It is not a great success and my fingers are getting chilly, but by tomorrow night we will be comfortable.

I will not be able to go to Tacoma this week. You don't know how sorry I am, but it is simply impossible. Shall I say that I am coming next week? Yes, I will and I hope to be able to see you then. Darling it seems an age. I hope this will reach you early enough so that you will not devote the whole of Saturday to expecting me.

Lovingly,
Hazen

Marysville Camp, Dec. 25, 1889

My Dearest,

I send a very merry Christmas for you. Was it a merry one? Why haven't I had a letter for some time? It has been a long time since I have heard from you ___ two weeks, I suppose. I trust you are enjoying your vacation very much at home, and I sincerely wish that I could have spent the day with you.

There is quite an unusual press of work now and that in connection with the estimate for December will keep me busy until the end of the month at least. I was sorely disappointed when I found that I couldn't well leave this week. It is quite impossible to name any day when I can go now, but I will certainly see you before the middle of next week.

It has been a beautiful day here, clear, cool and frosty. When are you going to write to me? Please give my kindest regards to your father and aunt, not forgetting your little sister.

Very much love,
Hazen

Dec. 26__ this morning I rec'd two letters from you which have been in Marysville for several days. I fail to see why they were not sent out as I rec'd other mail.

It was very nice of your school children to remember you so kindly. I wish I could kiss <u>almost</u> every one of them. I spent the day in a very improper way. First I mopped the floor, after

Carothers had swept it, and it needed it, I assure you. Then we fixed a door in our tent, which is quite an improvement on the old way of pinning the tent together.

Then I made some pigeon holes for the papers, which I had always found in the bottom of the stationery chest when I wanted them. And finally stopped work after making some improvements on my bed. It is half past eleven and raining. If it is not too bad I will go down the line seven miles tomorrow to do some necessary work. I hope to get the estimate done by Monday and other pressing work in such shape that Carothers can keep at it while I am away to then be with you ____ perhaps one day before the last of next week. Please do not let it interfere with any of your plans.

Lovingly,
Hazen

Snohamish, Wash., Jan. 5, 1890

My Darling____

Am I not very prompt? I am wondering if you had a safe and pleasant trip to Mr. Lee's. I have it figured out that you should arrive in Tacoma about the same time I took the train at Seattle and that you were safely under Mrs. Lee's kind care about the time I passed Union Bay____ Dearest, do you know what telltale eyes you have? When we were on the Fleetwood talking, they told me how much you cared for me, and how it hurt your dear heart to say "good bye"____

I am wondering if you think that I care as much for you? How can I tell you, love, but some time I think you will know that it is very much indeed and that I must depend upon your love for my strength in years to come.

Mr. Willard came out with me tonight. He is very pleasant and I must confess to a liking for him. I will go out to "camp one" very early in the morning, go to camp and push the work with might and main for a week.

I was up late last night and must retire. Perhaps you had better not keep such late hours as a steady practice. "Be good to my Emma."

Lovingly, Hazen

Seattle, May 14, 1890

My darling Emma,

I rec'd your delightful letter of Sunday last on going home yesterday evening. I intended to answer it at once but only got as far as the first three words, which was very good as far as it went but was hardly sufficient for a whole letter. I must have been troubled with biliousness, your recent enemy, for I haven't been very well today either.

If there had been a boat I would have been on my way to Lake McMurray, for I have to go up there to do a little work, and will undoubtedly be kept there over Sunday. I am half, no nine tenths vexed because I had intended to spend that day with you ____ if you've no objections ____ but if we can all go to Victoria on the 24th I will be highly delighted. I will try to convince Dickie that he must let me go, it will be quite a difficult undertaking, but if I am not out of town he will probably consent.

I saw Stixrud one day this week. He seems well pleased with his new work and wonders how he ever managed to stay out in the woods so long___ I wonder, too, for I wouldn't go back for anything.

Please give my kindest regards to our friends___

Lovingly,
Hazen

722 Madison St., May 20, 1890

My own Emma___

I returned from Lake McMurray this morning at 1 a.m. Mr. Nevins is away so I haven't been able to see him about the proposed trip to Victoria, but I shall try my very best to go and unless he has some R.R. surveys ready I think there will be no doubt about it. I would like very much to go as you have planned and would be grievously disappointed if anything occurred to prevent our going.

I will telegraph you not later than Friday night at 402 S. 28th St., before then if Nevins comes back. Why did I not find a letter tonight, love? I wanted one so very much.

Perhaps you have not fully recovered from your illness yet. Please be careful of "my Emma" ___won't you?

Tonight I went to call on your father and Myra but they were both out, so I came back as I had previously intended and wrote you. I am so sorry that I didn't go to see you tonight. I had intended to go to Tacoma on Sunday but the trip north spoiled that. Only one man went with me. The others I got from Mr. Wright at the lake. The work was finished by Saturday night, but no boat back until Monday so we remained at the camp the next day and went fishing____ very naughty, but it was the only thing we could do. Carothers declared that he was not coming here until the work was finished, but a month is all that I care to undertake of that kind of life, as you well know. Today I had a very good position offered me but I will probably decline. It was to take charge of a locating party in the Olympic Mountains. Darling, it may be very silly but I can't bear the thought of going away for several months and not see you at all during that time. I believe I prefer to remain where I am____ for really I must be married when I go to stay as long as that.

On what boat are we going and when does it leave Tacoma for Victoria?

Lovingly,
<u>*Hazen*</u>

722 Madison St., Thursday 10 P.M.
My own Emma,

This is the first opportunity I have had for writing and I gladly improve it, for it already seems a long time since I have seen you. I easily caught the Northern Pacific train Sunday night, and after coming here I went to the "Baily" and retired for the night. It was about one o'clock Monday when we reached Fir, for Mr. Wright, the man who takes my place, the rod man and a new cook were along. We walked over to camp where we found Mr. Carothers just in from his days work. It rather smote me to tell him that I was going away because I believe he went there only because he felt under obligations to me for having given him work on previous occasions. On Tuesday I went with W. over the line. He has never before had charge of any work and I consider Mr. Carothers much more capable at the present time. Yesterday Warner came to show my successor other features of the work so I felt that I was no longer under any obligation to remain and having packed up I started down the trail toward the supply camp which is on the road to Stanwood. It rained and the trail was very muddy, then it kept on raining and I met the boys on their way back to camp, said goodbye to them. They were kind enough to say they were sorry that I was going. Then I took a look at the lake with the uncouth cabins and clearings hidden from view and it is a lake which should have a better name than the one it wears, for the first man who looked at it must have beheld a gem. Then it rained as I started down the crooked trail for the last time. If I ever see it again how much it will be changed. The work now only begun will be finished and little farms will soon appear to the passenger looking from the car window.

Mr. Porter, the bookkeeper, welcomed me cordially at the supply camp where I stayed the last night. This morning I walked to Stanwood and waited until three o'clock this p.m. for the boat, reaching here at nine. This is my first offence with a pencil and you will please pardon it. I think you can write me here.

With very much love,
Hazen

Seattle, Wash. May 22, 1890

My dearest Emma:

Yours of Monday's date reached me yesterday. So we will celebrate the Queen's birthday in some other way. I will try to leave here on the 4:30 p.m. boat Saturday and will arrive in Tacoma about seven, early enough to go to the top of that high hill on which you dwell.

I was much interested in your account of your doings for the past week, and read your dear letter more than once. By Saturday it will have been three weeks since I have made my usual visit to you and the _rest_ of the Lee's, and it seems a year.

I haven't read the morning paper yet so you see that I cannot have very much information to write. How would you like to have me go out the Straits beyond Port Angeles and then through the Olympic Mountains? To Gray's Harbor, coming back in the fall? No fear____.

Will see you soon, dearest_

Lovingly,
Hazen

The many letters from Hazen to Emma came with even greater frequency. He came into Tacoma fairly often for supplies and always made it a point to see Thomas at his shop and inquire about Emma. Thomas often brought Hazen home with him for supper and sometimes overnight, but Emma was teaching on Vashon Island and missed nearly all of these occasions.

On one of the nights Thomas brought Hazen home, however, Emma was there and was delighted to see Hazen come with her papa. After supper the two young people sat together in the swing Thomas had hung on the porch outside when warm weather arrived. They swung back and forth for quite awhile in silence before Hazen turned to Emma.

"Emma, I have something to say to you . . ." he began.

"All right, Mr. Pratt." She turned on the swing so they were facing each other. She smiled and waited.

"Emma, I'm probably not doing this right, even though I should be when I'm saying something as important as this," he began.

"Oh, my goodness, Mr. Pratt . . ."

Hazen plunged ahead before she could finish.

"Emma . . . will you marry me?"

She hesitated barely a few seconds. Her eyes glowed, her smile was genuine, "Oh, yes, Mr. Pratt, yes!"

Hazen had his arms around her, holding her tight against him, his face buried in her hair.

"I must be the happiest man on earth, Emma! You are my whole world. You mean absolutely everything to me," he murmured.

"And I am the happiest woman on earth because you, dear Mr. Pratt, mean absolutely everything to me."

722 Madison St., June 27, 90 _
*My Darling Emma_*
I found your letter here when I returned Friday night for I didn't get away from Tacoma until 7:45 in the evening of that day. Once I thought it would be necessary to stay until Saturday morning and was on the point of sending a message boy to see if you would care for a drive, but it proved fortunate that I did not, for they finally concluded to send me back Friday night. I will be quite busy for two or three days and on the mudflats and then if I am not put on the Belt R.R. at once, will have an easy time of it.

I can hardly wait for your work to end and the coming week will seem a long one I fear.

I had a narrow escape last night. Yesterday morning Mrs. Hawley asked me if I had an engagement for last night. Completely forgetting myself, I said "no." Then she proceeded to order me to accompany Vonnie and a friend of hers to a temperance meeting or something of the kind. I wasn't highly pleased although I appeared to be and studied the remainder of the day how I might avoid it, and think I did it very cleverly.

A raft of piling had been brought here from Tacoma and the Capt. of the Tug thought he couldn't deliver it where I wanted it, so after supper I went with him up the river and among the rows of piles which are driven on the flats I found a place for him to go. He brought me back before eight o'clock, but I didn't appear at the house until this afternoon.

I heard today that Stixrud had been forced out of his position on the Waterworks because a man was wanted who could scheme and manipulate the City Council. I saw him a few minutes ago but he said nothing about it. He will probably go to the Great Northern.

I rec'd. a letter from Lizzie last week in which she said something very sweet about you. I am sure you would care very much for her if you knew her, for she is a sweet girl. I will write her today. I have been thinking that perhaps I will be living in camp next fall. Isn't that a prospect for you? I should think you would accept the place you are now leaving for good, rather than marry a man who will be living in a cloth house and who owns no other. How will it be____

I meant to have talked with Mrs. Lee but neglected it until too late. Tell her that I hope we didn't keep her awake.

Lovingly,
Hazen.

Seattle, Sept. 10, 1890

My Dearest,

Did I catch the train? Oh yes, and several minutes to spare as it leaves at 9:45 now. So I waited fifteen minutes, which a short time before would have been considered very precious time indeed. The train was delayed at Puyallulp so it was one o'clock when we reached our final stopping place. While Mr. Wright and Carothers were out Madison St. Sunday afternoon I read Ingersall's article on Tolstoi in the North American Review. I believe it is the best thing on the strange Russian I have ever read and you can have but one opinion and that is that he is on the subject of his much talked of book, an impracticable crank. The great atheist says beautiful love, marriage and home; and the contrast is so great between his healthy thoughts and those of "The Nightmare," that we must believe that the latter shows us only a "kind of insanity, nature soured and withered."

I will show the piece to you . . . no I will send it, for I cannot see you for two weeks. Is it unkind to say it ___ of course it is best___ but on looking at your letter again I find what you really say is that we must protract this kind of existence for a year. Perhaps you do not mean it, but if you have thought it best, please tell me all about it, won't you, Emma?

I have often thought that I am too morose and gloomy to mar your sweet life, but I am selfish enough to think that I cannot exit after once caring for you as I do, without your love to remain with me until the end. Is it selfish? I fear that I do not invite confidences although I am sure that you will readily believe that I do care for you.

Stixrud wants me to go to Tacoma on Saturday with him so you may see me if it isn't two weeks, but he does not yet know whether the court is in session or not.

Last night I was preparing a letter to Mr. Hudson regarding a "kick" which Reynolds is making against me. I have no idea that it will be serious as I am sure I will have no trouble in convincing Mr. H. that Reynolds is trying to work off poor material. I have an instrument now, and after a few days, will have considerable leisure time.

I began a letter to you on Sunday but somehow could not finish it.

Very much love,
<u>*Hazen*</u>

Squire-Lattimer Bldg.
Room 59,
Seattle, Sept. 16, 1890

My dearest Emma,

Thinking there might be a letter for me I went to my room on my way to dinner and found it. I have also been anxiously looking for a letter from home. As yet I haven't it. As Arthur will have to start within a week from the present time in order to reach here before his pass expires, I will soon hear from him, as I wrote him to write me a few days before he started.

A short time ago it occurred to me that he had said nothing about coming since the first of the summer, and the last letter from Lizzie came before you went to Tacoma, so I am not perfectly sure that he is still in favor of coming, but I would think it foolish of him to back out, when he can come so cheaply and spend the winter here, which is very much milder than a Vermont winter, and then if he chose, go back again.

I looked for Mr. Stixrud Saturday morning but didn't see him and as he hasn't expressed a desire to go soon, I will let him choose his own time. Of course that accounts for my staying here although I wished myself with you more than once.

Oh, I haven't told you that I have moved from the depot. It was very much crowded there and I only had desk room, while here I have two rooms and everything in proper shape. It is on Commercial St. nearly opposite the New England Hotel.

I have an Instrument man now and much of the drudgery is taken off my hands. It has been very smoky here, too, so that we couldn't do instrument work at all. Today West Seattle and Queen Anne town are visible although it is still quite smoky and I hope the boys will succeed in catching up.

I have seen nothing I want to send Will and am in a terrible dilemma. I thought some of getting him a bearskin rug, something like yours, but have seen none nice enough. Perhaps something in silver would be better but I never can trust myself to select it. Find it in Tacoma and I will get it there and give you a kiss for your pains, and duplicate it for you when you get married. So be sure that it is nice enough.

If the weather is at all clear on Saturday I will not go to Tacoma until Sunday morning, probably leaving here on the 9:25 train. Shall we peruse that North American Review?

It already seems a month since I have seen you, and I am on the point of declaring this two weeks business a nuisance.

Lovingly,
Hazen.

722 Madison St., Sept 30, '90
My dearest Emma,
So you went by boat, at such an hour, too. Please don't do it again for you are liable to take cold, and I think your work at Tacoma is sufficient tax on your health and strength. Pardon me for talking to you as I would to Lizzie, but you must admit that it is so.

I went down to the 6:10 train and thought you had certainly missed it. You see I was trying to show you that I could get up, but you were too early for me.

I rec'd Will's wedding cards today and suppose you did too. We hope they will be happy, as of course they will, for Will needs a wife to look after him and keep him from working nineteen hours a day, and I believe he is a man who would make a good woman very happy. Yesterday morning we sent the cinnamon bear skin, and when I looked at it this time I thought it quite handsome.

Arthur and I went out to the head of the bay today and he got quite tired. He is anxious to begin work but I do not think I will let him do much except to familiarize himself with some portions of it. Then I hope he will be stronger, and at the same time know more about the work. He is very quick to pick it up and I wish I had enough office work to keep him busy about two thirds of the time and let him go out the remainder. I intended to write you this morning but put it off too long. We will hope that the Lees will be fortunate enough to go to Gig Harbor. I am relying upon you to tell Mr. Lee that there is no immediate prospect of work here.

We are about to try a boarding house on Second St. I fear Artie will have a hard time of it, for I should starve to death on what he eats.

I hope you are not ill after your morning boat ride. Many kisses and much love,

Hazen___

722 Madison St., Nov. 4, 1890

My darling Emma,

It was too bad that we couldn't go home when we ought, and I discovered early in the evening how tired you were. I really felt quite ashamed knowing as I did what a long day it had been for you. Perhaps it was Miss Lovell's intense earnestness in the rubber and the desire on my part to help her all I could. You see I am trying to shift the responsibility on to someone else, or shall I tell you while I held the cards in my hands I could also look up and see you.

But I am rather glad we won that last game, aren't you? You and Mr. Mallory would have talked ever so much more about it than we did, wouldn't you?

I didn't take the early train but waited and spent an hour in the N. P. Building.

Thanks to the good help D. had last night the estimate is finished. Valentine made two copies this afternoon. I am greatly relieved for it represents nearly a week of work.

Walter came yesterday. They went to Juanita this morning so I haven't seen him yet. I almost regret going back there for Arthur is not as well as he was when he boarded elsewhere. The climb up the hill is one reason I suppose. There is steam heat in the office at last and I think now we will be comfortable there.

Do you know that I am sorry we were not married this fall? It sounds very reckless, but life is almost a burden when I am away from you, and we would be so happy. I am not demonstrative. I wish I were. But I love you very much, Emma, while perhaps you may know even if I haven't told you as often as I should. Do you believe we should have been so rash? Did you discover that I was awfully blue Saturday night? I couldn't help it. Although I regretted it very much as I haven't had enough sleep lately. I will improve the chance, which I feel sure you are doing.

Remember me to Miss Lovell.

Dearest, Good Night.

Your very own,
Hazen

Chapter Twelve

*T*he holidays were over and Emma was back at school teaching before Hazen's first letter of the new year of 1891 reached her. It was written on a sheet of paper from the

"Northern Pacific Railroad Company, Construction Department"

150 Squire St. - Latimer Bldg., Jan.7, 1891

My Dearest___
Your letter came in the morning and all other business was dropped as usual, until I read it___ and wandered mentally back to be with you.

I fear the screen did not progress at all while Mr. Mallory was there, and it is very evident to me that Miss Lovell and I will have it to finish. However, I shall find it one of the pleasantest of tasks, and if it is not finished in one evening it will be because we appreciate the extreme nicety of the work and intend to do it justice. I am not surprised at our friends sudden change of front___ when will the next one take place?

I had five minutes to spare after stopping to buy a package of Spanish cigarettes. They are not at all like the American kind ___ so much better that I would send you one only I wouldn't like to have you get into the habit of smoking.

Miss Knowles and Mrs. Hawley are going to Cordage tonight. What a delightful dose of gunpowder smoke they will get. Should any good company come to Tacoma you would like to see or hear, you know that I will be more than delighted to go over to accompany you. My kindest regards to all of those schoolteachers who sent their love to me some time ago.

Hazen

722 Madison St., Jan. 13, '91

My Dearest Emma___

Last night I was in Tacoma until 10:30. A letter had failed to bring a transit, which was needed here very much . . . so I went for it. Perhaps 'twould be plainer to say that I left it at the 17th St. station Saturday afternoon and actually forgot it Sunday morning. If you would like to laugh at me you may. I sent you a copper teakettle instead of calling to see you, as I had been there so recently, and having just read that "a man in love is a nuisance" I managed to steer myself to the hotel. I hope you will like it__ the teakettle, I mean, but please don't say so unless you do__ for in time you might cultivate a better taste in me, and I would take anything you might say with such good nature that it would surely surprise you.

I can change the whole arrangement much easier than Nellie Bly did her manicure set, and get a different design for a stand.

How foggy it was in your village last night. I pretended to read but my thoughts travelled off up the hill and I saw you busying yourself with books and papers and small talk with your friends.

We have actually found a new boarding place and partaken of three meals nicely cooked and served. When I came back Sunday Arthur was as cross as a bear about our former one, and showed me a list of "ads," any of which he seemed to think preferable to our present place. So I made a list of four of the most eligible ones and we took a walk to examine their exterior. One on Marion St. opposite the Methodist Church seemed convenient and I stopped on my way down town yesterday morning. It's a nice place where it would be only Dr. Newland and us. Arthur has recovered his good nature, and I am not surprised. I think you would say that it surpassed our favorite restaurant.

Mrs. Jasper, the wife of one of the resident engineers on the Belt line was in the office today. What do you think, love, she is cooking for the party instead of having a man. Carothers told me they were "hard up" when he got the position, and I suppose that accounts for it. Isn't that too bad.

It was after one when I went to bed this morning so I must turn in early.

Very much love from
Your very own Hazen

Friday Evening, Jan. 16, 1891

My Darling___

Your letter came yesterday___ it was so like you that I wanted to kiss it, but I didn't because there were so many men around. It seemed to remind me that it and you, love, were absolutely necessary to my existence, and I believe you are, don't you? Another vexations estimate was required yesterday on the shortest possible notice and after working late last night I have just finished it. It seems the company is hard up, and they wanted to know how much it would cost to finish up the work, which is started, without finishing the whole work as it was originally planned. $25,000 is the amount required and the end of March is the time I have estimated to have it completed. The Belt Line is ordered to be stopped at the "steel works" at Kirkland. A proposition was made to me one day this week about building a house and it started me to wondering if it would be a wise plan. So I must tell you although I do not expect you to approve of it, exactly.

Mr. Parker, an Episcopal Clergyman has a sawmill, house and some other property at Green Lake. At present he is cutting timber that we are using here in Seattle. Strange business for a man of cloth to be engaged in isn't it? Well, he told me that Judge Wood was going to give away some lots on the condition that they were built upon and Mr. Parker said he would give me the timber if I wanted it___ lumber I mean___ to build a house. That seems strange for a man to be so generous, doesn't it, but I can explain to you something about how that came about. I believe you know Judge Wood so you see I would have two pleasant neighbors.

What a pity that I didn't read your Tacoma papers and find out about the lecture Monday evening, for I would have known that you would be glad to even listen to a man say "Siberia." It is almost a selfish motive, but we read about it once, and I wouldn't have been killing time alone.

I will prize the lock of hair above everything. Strange as it may seem, it is the only one that I can reckon among my treasures.

Has the piano arrived yet? Miss Lovell and I will play duets next time. Please give her my kindest regards. It is late and I must go home. Will I get a letter tomorrow? I hardly know what to do between Saturday and Monday when I am not to go to see you.

Be a good girl, and write to me. Ten thousand kisses___

Your Hazen

Jan. 23, 1891

My Love,

I reached the train all right and had one minute to spare, so I could have walked a trifle slower, no I mean I could have staid one minute longer with you. It was too bad to come away last night when you were so good as to make tea for us, but I am sure the others appreciated it as well as I did and some time I will partake of it, but I thought I had better come last night. I tried very hard to go over Wednesday evening, but was doing something for Mr. Estep, which kept me busy until half past six, an hour after the train left, that accounts for my not writing then. I will leave here at 9:15 Sunday morning and will be sure to have my breakfast here for Mrs. Newman's breakfasts are dainty and nice. Her lunches are simple but extremely nice. The Dr.'s father arrived from Kingston, Canada this morning and gave them an agreeable surprise. He is a good specimen of one of Her Majesty's subjects, but his son has become thoroughly Americanized.

There was a funny old pair on the train coming from Puyallup to Seattle last night. They had just arrived from Dakota and intended locating at Sultan City. The feminine half of the pair was a great strange coarse woman who could hold a plow or wield a hoe among her accomplishments and her voice was as strange as the rest of her. She kept the poor man in perfect terror and so far exceeded anything in "Widow Bedatt," "Spoopendyke" or Samantha Allen that she kept a car full of people highly entertained. And she was so severe on her *poor man that it didn't seem at all mean for the brakemen to chaff her, which they did to their hearts' content.*

I forgot to call your attention to an account of the city council in the Telegraph*. A committee, which has been investigating Stixrud's bill, declares it to be just and that he is entitled to the amount demanded. This bill is a very few dollars larger than the one the Board of Public works refused to approve when they dismissed him, so we can see the there was a great deal of injustice in their actions, as I surmised.*

Goodbye dearest I must go to the lunch I have been dilating about. How long a time it seems before I can see you. Until Sunday.

Lovingly your
Hazen

I have your pencil___

Emma and Hazen decided on a quiet wedding right in her papa's home, with Hazen's brother Arthur there as a witness. Arthur was delighted to be able to be there as their witness. They chose April 14th of that year of 1891 as their wedding date.

The two brothers came to Tacoma to Thomas Clarke's home on the 14th of April, bearing bottles of wine to open after the vows were said. It was to be a real celebration as Hazen was at last taking the big step of marriage. Hazen had been extremely close to becoming a confirmed bachelor at thirty-three. He had been more than a little afraid Emma would think the nine-year age difference between them was too much, but age proved to be immaterial to her. She loved him and that was all that mattered. Hazen was an immensely happy man.

The minster spoke the words, phrase by phrase, which Hazen and Emma repeated after him, the words that committed them each to the other.

"I, Hazen, take thee, Emma, to be my wedded wife, to have and to hold from this day forward, for better for worse, for richer for poorer, in sickness and in health, to love and to cherish, till death us do part, according to God's holy ordinance; and thereto I plight thee my troth.

"I, Emma, take thee, Hazen, to be my wedded husband, to have and to hold from this day forward, for better or for worse, for richer or for poorer, in sickness and in health, to love, and to cherish, till death us do part, according to God's holy ordinance; and thereto I give thee my troth."

Hazen turned to Arthur. Arthur withdrew the ring from his pocket and gave it to Hazen. Then Hazen repeated the rest of the phrases after the minister.

"With this ring I thee wed, with my body I thee worship, and with all my worldly goods I thee endow: In the name of the Father, and of the Son, and of the Holy Ghost. Amen."

Emma repeated, "Amen."

The minister's final words brought smiles to all of them.

"Those whom God has joined together, let no man put asunder. I now pronounce you husband and wife. Hazen, you may kiss your bride."

Hazen bent to kiss his bride, holding her close. He reluctantly released her and turned to Arthur.

"May I present Mrs. G. Hazen Pratt?"

Arthur laughed. "You may." He turned to Emma. "Welcome to the family, Mrs. Pratt."

"I am happy to become a member of your family, Mr. Arthur Pratt." Emma smiled at Arthur, but was completely surprised when Arthur turned to Hazen, "May I kiss the bride?"

Hazen laughed, "You may . . . but just this once."

The kiss was bestowed and soon they were all laughing and congratulating the new couple. The wine was opened and toasts were given. It was the happiest of days for Emma and Hazen.

Arthur Eugene Pratt

Chapter Thirteen

*T*he first year of marriage for Emma and Hazen went by quickly, or so it seemed to them, for Emma became pregnant shortly after the wedding. There was much to do before the baby came. Hazen was away a good bit of the time surveying and Emma was left alone. She moved back to live with her papa when the time came near for the baby to arrive. It was Thomas who located the midwife for help and it was Thomas who paced the floor as Emma labored to give birth to her first little girl . . . and Thomas's first grandchild. There had been no way to let Hazen know Emma was about to deliver the sweet baby that she and Hazen later named Ruth Elizabeth.

Hazen rented a small cottage in Woodinville where he thought Emma might feel more at ease because of her having lived and taught school there a few years back.

"You'll know the people in Woodinville which will help you feel more at ease when I can't be with you, Emma."

"You are right . . . and . . . you are so thoughtful of me." She smiled up at him with love written all over her face.

"And that, my dear, is because of how much I love you." He reached for her and held her in his arms, his face in her hair as he talked.

Emma clung to him, then almost tearfully, "But I shall miss you most dreadfully. Baby and I need our papa."

"I know. I know. I can come more often now, though . . . now that you are nearer to where I'm working."

Emma made no reply but continued to stay close in his arms.

Hazen's first letter to her came shortly after he had left Woodinville.

421 Madison St., Mar. 23

My Dearest,

I got to town Friday about 8:30 thanks to your early breakfast. Berglund and I have been working yesterday and today and by Monday we will be thoroughly in the harness again. I don't know yet when the warrants will appear. Kiehl thought in about a week.

The town has been very much excited over the capture of Blanck. *His pictures and wooden gun are on exhibition and a great many people have been to the undertakers to see him.*

I am rooming and boarding at Mr. Truax and it seems very pleasant, but I miss my wife and baby. I slept from nine until seven last night so you see I am improving my time. Mr. Truax still has his cough, but the others are nearly as well as usual.

I will go out and see Myra tomorrow, and I will write Will and Lizzie. It has been quite squally here until this afternoon. I hope we will get settled weather soon.

If you are not going to use that box of earth you had sweet peas in, you might get the gardener next door to bring it up and you could put some tomato seed in it. Have him put it upstairs on the trunk in front of the window. I'm afraid "Berg's" seeds will not grow good out of doors in all this wet. Peterson has part of a paper of tomato seed Berglund brought. The potato rows are to be 3 1/2 ft. apart if you can get the gardener's help.

I hope you are getting along all right.

How is baby? She will have to talk to you if you are going to stay alone very much. Better arrange to get a gallon of milk on Sunday and Wednesday or any time when convenient, but get it regularly. I love you,

Hazen

Lake Stevens, Nov. 8, 1892

My Darling_____

I got your Sunday evening letter today while over at Hartford for the purpose of voting. The Grangers made me swear in my vote because my wife lived in Seattle. But I was sure I had a voting residence here and so I voted to keep even with my voting wife in Seattle.

I am sorry I couldn't take the ride with you and Baby and Mrs. Merriam. Perhaps I will just before Thanksgiving Day. I will probably be through here within two weeks.

Artie's address is 929 E. St., Tacoma. I wish you would write him and ask him over. Tell him to come prepared to stay the rest of the week. If I am not through here I will bring him out, and if I am, I will arrange to have him sleep at Mrs. Benson's or somewhere else.

I don't think I can come home next Sunday. Will probably have the preliminary work in that direction done so that I can project some new location, but I will be down near Marysville and if I can get away when the train comes along I may step on. Who is going to be the next president?

Your darling is well and in tolerable spirits. I got that kiss.

Lovingly,
Hazen

Snohomish, Wash.,
Tuesday Eve.
Dec. 13, 1892

My Dearest,

I found your very welcome letter of the 11th here when I came in tonight. I am delighted to think you have recovered from your cold. Please do as I did and get yourself some warm under vests for you need them quite as much as I did. I think a person in this country needs as warm clothing at this time of the year as they do in Vermont for instance. Don't you?

Mr. Relf came into the office last night and cheered me with the news that he had seen you that very day. I am glad Petty Pratt is getting old enough to help amuse Petty Pratt, herself. You will not need to carry her about so much when she can creep. I thought I should be able to get home to stay by this time and see her grow but since I came back from Marysville Sunday night Mr. Fisher has put me to staking out a gravel pit. Will finish it tomorrow. Mr. Berman, the draughtsman who has been making maps of the Lake Stevens line, hurt his back and is not yet able to go to work, so while I am waiting the Chief will keep me working on small jobs like this. He told me tonight that he would be through with me by the end of the week, so I don't suppose you will see me before Saturday.

We can go out to the ranch some time next week. This winter while I am at home I must go out and make you a kitchen where there is now only a roof, and put a heating stove in the cabin and fix it up a bit.

I am stopping in a private house this time and really sleeping in John Folstad's bed while he has gone to Seattle. You see the room was vacant when I was here before and I went there expecting to get it for a few days but J.J. had moved in in the meantime and offered to share it with me, so I surprised him by saying I would, but in the evening I go in to see Mr. Berglund and smoke a pipe with him.

I am so anxious to get home again and live with my sweetheart that I almost feel hurt when Mr. Fisher says he has a few more days work for me.

Mr. Carothers came in awhile last night. I presume you have noticed that he has been elected County Surveyor. Times are pretty dull with him at present I think.

Last night I left a window open near my bed and by morning I was wondering if the skating was good on the river. While out on the line last week I had taken cold, so I am weeping and sneezing now.

Love to our little girl and much for yourself.

Your loving husband,
Hazen

Hazen's reference to "the ranch" in his letter amused Emma as that was what he called the land she had homesteaded. Now that Emma was living in Woodinville he came home more often as he loved their little Ruth and enjoyed spending time with her and, of course, time with her mother. The baby had made rapid progress and was able to stand beside

Emma, clutching her skirt. They were both so proud of her.

"How are my sweethearts today," was Hazen's greeting when he walked in the door. One of the times he came asking that same question Emma looked concerned.

"Little Ruth is not feeling very well, Hazen. I don't know what it is. She is just so listless and I can't interest her in anything."

"We'd better get a doctor."

They did call a doctor who diagnosed little Ruth with peritonitis for which he could offer no help. Emma and Hazen were devastated as they watched their little angel slowly slip away from them.

After baby Ruth passed away and was buried Emma turned to Hazen.

"Hazen, I must go back to teaching. I absolutely cannot stay home here alone without our baby."

"I know, dear. I know. It's all right. Do whatever you feel is best."

So with Hazen's approval Emma was back teaching again, filling her days with the needs of other people's children. She worked for a couple of years before she became pregnant again.

Emma went into labor one cold January morning of 1895. This time Hazen was at home. It was Hazen who paced the floor outside the room where Emma labored instead of Emma's papa Thomas. Hazen was delighted to learn the new baby was another little girl. Together they immediately named her Dorothy.

Hazen's letters resumed again. Emma smiled when she saw his salutation of "My Dear Polly." She checked his closing. He had changed that, too. "Ah, that man," she muttered under her breath, still smiling, however. He had so carefully reminded her that his name was actually George Hazen Pratt and that perhaps she should begin calling him George. She continued calling him "Mr. Pratt." The "Polly" was part of his little joke from when they were together and it was time for tea. He would sing to her, "Polly, put the kettle on and we'll all have tea."

She missed Hazen terribly when he was away. His absences would be totally unbearable if it weren't for his frequent dear letters to her.

Seattle, March 27, 1895.

*My Dear Polly*_____

Three years ago today my Polly was suffering extreme anguish all alone, and before a year had passed our pet had left us. If this one will only stay with us, how happy we will be.

Your letter came Monday morning and I was glad to hear you were both well. I haven't been to see Myra yet but sent her $10 at the University, with a promise of more next week. How warm it is and how it rains! Those early peas will soon sprout in this weather.

Mr. Smith is going to move into one of the Hathaway houses this week, he told me yesterday, so I put an "ad" in today's paper. Fred Gasch, County Commissioner, was the first applicant and I may let him have it. Another man wanted to get it for the Unitarian minister and was very anxious to get it at $25, but I firmly refused at that price. Smith owes for March yet. I hope I can get a good tenant.

The Truax family are well as usual. Florence is quite a pretty girl, if she will only cultivate the right qualities.

McFee came in the other day. He said he thought his brother was going to send back east for syrup. I haven't seen anyone else.

Had quite a long talk with Mr. Merriam last night. He said Mrs. M. would go out about May 1st.

Mr. Kiehl told me that they would need a nurse soon and asked who you had. Please send me the *number of Mrs. Kelly's P.O. Box. What did Mrs. Merriam pay her?*

1894 taxes become delinquent Saturday night. I'm afraid the Insurance check will not come until next week. Mr. Stixrud said Prasch told him the Governor had just signed the deficiency bill and that the warrants would come <u>sometime</u>. Give my regards to Peterson and Dilly.

> *A kiss for Baby,*
> *My best love for your dear self,*
> *George*

Chapter Fourteen

*M*ore letters from Hazen found their way to Woodinville. Hazen was a faithful letter writer and Emma was grateful.

Seattle, March 30,1895.

My Dearest Wife_____
I went out and saw Myra Thursday night and saw her baby for the first time. From what Mrs. Spikes says, she has a good deal of colic and cries some. I asked Myra how much money she would need but she didn't tell me.

Taxes are not delinquent until May 31st, then half are due and the other half Nov. 1st. Isn't that a relief? The warrant came yesterday.

I'm afraid that I won't be able to rent the house this month. Very few people have applied as far as I know. I hoped Mr. Gasch would take it but he didn't come back again. The Unitarian minister can pay only $25. I don't want to take that. Two ladies came. One wanted a window cut in the north side of the front room upstairs. Of course I told her that I couldn't do that, and she wanted the same room papered. It really looks as well as any room in the house now, but as she didn't seem to care about the back rooms I said I would paper it, but she must have had her heart set on the window for I haven't seen her since. She ought to have had more sense. The other one didn't want it rebuilt, but I apprehend it was too much of a house for her. She said her husband was manager of the Pt. Gamble Mill. I didn't think we would have such difficulties, but perhaps it would be different if someone else were there besides Smith. Anyway, we are getting rid of Smith. It makes me sick to think we must lose a month's rent.

Myra said Prof. Johnson had had a fainting spell. Mrs. Johnson was afraid he might be dying and asked some of the neighbors to come in and help her. When "O.B." came to himself he was upset and angry to see all the other people about.

Myra also said Grace Lee called at the University to see her on Monday. The gushing girl said she was to be married in three weeks to a man who is to have the "Domestic" business in MacD. & S., in fact the gentleman was over that day to see about it and Grace came with him.

I am writing in Stixrud's office after supper so I can mail it tonight and make sure of its going tomorrow. What kind of a week have you had? I hope everything goes well. Berglund and I will work half a day tomorrow. Unless more help is put on we will be here until the 15th, I should think.

Give Dorothy a kiss or two and hug yourself for me. I would like to see you, but if I can earn two dollars instead perhaps I had better do it.

Very much love,
George

The cabin built on Emma's homesteaded property had had numerous things done to it through her years with Hazen and the two of them laughingly named it "Fool's Paradise." Summers between school years were usually spent there. They planted crops in the early spring and harvested them before school convened again in the fall.

Fools Paradise 1895

Hazen kept close contact with his only sister Lizzie (Elizabeth Roxanne Pratt) with letters back and forth. He was concerned about her and had been begging her to come to Washington. He was delighted when she finally made the big decision to come west.

Elizabeth Roxanne Pratt

Seattle,
Friday evening.

My Dearest Polly,
How are you all getting on? I am afraid you are doing too much "hard work," Mama. I estimate there will be some plowing done tomorrow around Fool's Paradise. I should think the guano ought to be used on the potatoes and put in the hill. I suppose Mr. P. will take out a shovel full of earth as usual, then the stuff can be put in, a big spoonful or so. If his own work is pressing he had better get

someone to help him on ours. Better have him plant the peas, too.

I began work as soon as I got here and have been steadily at it since, evenings, too. Last night I wrote to Lizzie. She can come on the C.P.R. for about $70, . . . that is tourist. By the N.P. it is a little more, and I am afraid the accommodations are not as good. The time is 5 1/2 days. The agent here said the car (C.P.) went over the Central Vermont and actually came to Seattle. I advised Lizzie to come prepared to stay a year. I saw the paper today that many of the roads had made no special rates, and if they do I am afraid they will put too short a limit on her stay here to suit us.

I board at Mrs. Coleman's. She wishes to be remembered to you and says you must come to Seattle while I am here. She has a cold at present but is otherwise much better than she was in the winter.

How is my Dorothy? Much love to you all,

George

*Camp #3,
Five miles N. of Barlow Pass
Sunday, July 25.*

My Dearest Emma____

This was a fine day here and Devault and I spent the most of it fishing. We got forty and they were all of fair size and some beauties. I got one 15 inches long, about a two pounder. I wish you could have seen it. I got one almost like it the other night. The road along which we are working follows the river so our camping places are convenient to pretty good fishing. On Tuesday we will move three miles further down the river to a small settlement called Orient in Twp. 30N R11E. I believe there are two families living there. They will be the first settlers we will pass. The road is washed away in several places so that it is only available for pack animals or riding. We are thankful that we have no mountain to climb. We will probably keep on until we reach Darrington in Twp. 32N R9E about opposite the head of the N. fork of the Stillaquamish. We had some wet weather last week. I wonder if the haying is done. You would like to see the mountains up here. Of course we don't have the chance to see scenery such as some of the men who have climbed the peaks before have. The peaks rise on each side of the river a thousand feet or more . . . steep and precipitous . . . with many fine waterfalls tumbling down them. This camp is about nine miles from Monte Cristo and 1,000 feet lower. We have a new cook now and a good one.

Is Ethel with you? And how are you getting on?
I send my love to Dorothy Pratt and her mama.
I wish I could see you both.

George

Camp #7 -
One mile below White Chuck Creek

My Dear Wife . . .
A man came down from Monte Cristo today so I am taking the chance to send a letter, for the next P.O. is Darrington down near the head of the N. fork of Stillaquamish. From Darrington we will do down to near Oso on the N. fork and stop, but that may take the rest of this month. The weather is fine. The land around the river is all taken up along here but the most of the settlers are away. This is comparatively low country about 900 ft. above the sea, while Monte Cristo is about 2760.
Have rec'd your letter enclosing Effie's. You had better direct mail to Darrington, Snohomish Co. for the next three weeks. I don't think we will hear from above often now. Don't know how often Darrington gets mail, but probably twice a week.
Three other men are already in bed so I'll have to stop.

Lovingly,
George

The next letter Emma had from Hazen was written on small pages of stationery from the Hotel Monte Cristo, Everett, Washington.

Sunday Eve., July 4, 1897
My Dearest Polly,
I will go back to Monte Cristo in the morning . . . was copying notes from the old construction books until late yesterday afternoon. Yesterday Mr. Fletcher

wired me to get another level, so last night I took the Greyhound back to Seattle. It was half past ten when I reached Mrs. Coleman's but they were up and I staid there, and got a level from S. & N. for a few days.

Today we took a sail and were out from ten till one and had a breeze the most of the time.

Mrs. Coleman and Nasten still have it hot and heavy. Nasten really ought to keep quiet. I think Ethel will soon be ready to go out and see you. It would please them all I think to have her go, particularly Mrs. Coleman.

It was so late when I got to Seattle that I didn't try to see the fireworks, they said they were very good the night before . . . neither did I see much here . . . the laying of the corner stone of the courthouse and bicycle race . . . only saw the canoe race as I went to take the boat. Eleven Indians in each canoe shoveled the water in a very lively way.

Is Miss Clohery married? She boards - lives - here at the hotel apparently but I haven't taken the trouble to introduce myself. In fact I look pretty tough to be starring it here among the swells. Write to Monte Cristo, c/o of U. S. Geological Survey.

Lovingly,
George

Department of the Interior
UNITED STATES GEOLOGICAL SURVEY

My post-office address is.... Monte Cristo, Wash.
My telegraph address is........Monte Cristo, Wash.
My express address is............... Monte Cristo, Wash.

Tuesday Eve., July 13, 1897

My Darling Wife___

I hope you reached home safely as no doubt you did. I guess you don't know how I hated to leave you, but we both are so glad that I have got some work that we won't mind that. I followed you in my mind all the way home, and wish I could see you this minute.

Tomorrow we leave the headquarters camp and move two or three miles down the Sauk River. I will continue to move about every other day and would not be surprised if I did not get back for three weeks, or more. Have two rodmen, John DeVault is one, and a packer with two ponies ___ the packer is supposed to cook when he isn't going back and forth on the trail, when we all take a hand in it. It will be roughing it, but as long as the weather is good I don't mind.

Mr. Fletcher went down the road today to Pilchuck Mt. He will climb it and put a signal on the summit. The other man had already gone on a similar trip when I returned from Seattle so I have the tent all to myself tonight. Have packed the things I will take along and while overhauling my clothes bag found the pkg. of wafers which Myra put in, and have just about finished the last one___ they are mighty good. Today Ethel comes out to see you____ and Mr. Bergland, too. I am glad you can have a little company now and then. What a nice present the music box was for Dorothy. When you go to Seattle you must have her picture taken.

Now, as she is two and a half years old, you must measure her height again. Tell her papa loves her.

Perhaps you had better write those people in Seattle when you will come for the rent. Mrs. Young at 1005 and Mrs. F. A. Boyd at 1007. I believe Mr. Glossup's rent is paid to June 11, and $1.00 on the next months besides. Tell them to get some one to do the papering. They were to pay for half of it____ and Mrs. G. said she would fix the cloth if it was sewed ____she is anxious to have it done cheaply. Oh dear, I wish that whole business was safely off our hands. The excursions from Seattle to this place have gone by way of Woodinville. The scenery from Silverton up is worth seeing.

It is late . . . after eleven, and I must unroll my blankets and get into them. Good night . . .

Lovingly,
George___

Camp #8 at mouth of Char Creek
S.W. Co T. 32 N. R 10 E.
August 10, 1897

My Dearest Emma_____

The above heading will show you where I am. You can extend the Twp. lines on the map. Char Creek is a fine stream about a hundred feet wide, and the water is beautifully clear with a greenish tint. On Sunday DeVault and I went a short distance up to try the fishing. The creek runs through a narrow canyon in the lower part of its course and we had to climb up and down and up again ____ *a precarious climb, too, for the walls are nearly perpendicular. A thunderstorm came up as we were climbing up the last time after having caught a dozen fine trout. The rain was not heavy but the thunder sounded like Rip Van Winkle ninepins.*

If the weather is favorable we will reach the vicinity of Darrington with the levels by Friday night ____ will move again Thursday. I believe I mentioned that we would run down the N. fork of the Stillaquamish into Tp. 32N.R7E . . . it will take the rest of this month. I make an average 1 1/5 miles per day.

Forgive me for stopping here. Tomorrow I will add more.

Hazen hadn't added to the letter and this partial letter was tucked in with a longer one he wrote later.

Camp 10
Sec 8T32N.R9E
Sunday, August 15 --

We left Char Creek on Thursday and reached Darrington that night with both camp and levels. Brown's horses ran off down the river with a band of Indians so he borrowed a horse of a prospector to move with. Darrington consists at present of two habitations, a cabin where some miners are living in Sc.24 of this Tp. and another house 1/2 mile further west, where the P.O. is. The mail is brought up from Arlington three times a week.

Darrington is on the E. edge of a sandy, gravely plain about four miles wide lying between some mountains running along the county line on the north (where the N. Fork of the Stillaquamish heads), and the White Horse Mountain on the S., the source of Squire and Ashton creeks. These streams join the Stillaquamish in the W. part of this section. This camp is on Squire Creek where the road, or trail rather, crosses it . . . such fine clear cold water . . . running down through the vine, maple, alder and cedar. It was a welcome contrast to the hot dry plain above. This plain is locally known as the "Burn." All of the timber except scattered bunches of scrub fir and pine has been destroyed by fire so it is comparatively bare, for this country. The heat is so intense at present during the day that we can work only in early morning and late in the afternoon. Yesterday was the first day it has bothered us. We had to stop at eleven o'clock and begin again at five. I hope to get across it tomorrow by beginning at daylight. Along the bottom the timber is thick enough so the heat does not interfere with the seeing ____ except where settlers have made clearings. White Horse Mountain is a grand peak 9,000 feet high. The top is inaccessible so far as known ____ the summit is bare rock with perpendicular sides ____ on the N.W. side of the summit at the foot of this sharp point is a glacier flowing off well from the "Burn." Several streams come tumbling down fed by the melting snow. If our datum is correct we are only 50 or 100 ft. higher here than "Fools Paradise." Isn't it hot there these days? You must be near melting.

How is Dorothy? What does she think of hot weather? I imagine I can see her running around in the shade of the house dodging out into the sun in spite of the heat. She is growing so fast that I'll be surprised, even if I'm not away very long. Wish I could see you all. Has Berglund gone back? Here's a kiss for you both.

Lovingly yours,
George

It was not long after Hazen's last visit that Emma learned she was pregnant again. She was delighted at the thought of a playmate for little Dorothy. She hadn't yet written to tell Hazen when she received his first letter.

"My goodness," Emma said to herself as she opened it, "he's written a book!" She sat down happily to read.

U. S. S. Wheeling, Behring Sea
Sunday, June 26, 1898____

My Dearest Emma____

We left Dutch Harbor at nine this morning and are steadily ploughing north. The bright weather came to an end last night. Today a light rain & moderate S.E. wind. Behring Sea is considered very quiet water but since lunch I notice we have some rolling about. From the tug New England, which came into Dutch Harbor yesterday from St. Michael, we learn that ice was still in the sea, but by following the edge of the mud flats near the mouth of the river they and other vessels have reached St. M. some time ago. Quite a number of vessels went up from Onualaska just before we got there. This morning the Steamer Samoa came in from San Francisco towing a river steamer. They had about 150 passengers. I suppose we will see a great array of people and craft at St. M. A good many boats and barges are being built at Onualaska and Dutch Harbor. There are four shipyards. Both these places are on the same bay or inlet separated by a narrow point of land. The first is the larger and I believe is as old as Sitka. There have been a few buildings there for years, but excepting the Russian Church, customs house, and courthouse. The Alaska Commercial Co. seems to own the place. This was the company with the lease of the Seal Islands until a few ears ago. Now the North American Commercial Co. has the lease and they have their buildings, wharf, etc. at Dutch Harbor. Mr. Stanley-Brown, who married one of President Garfield's daughters, is the Company's Agent here. The Wheeling took on $750 worth of their coal and bought beef at 25 cents per pound.

Yesterday Judge Wood lunched with the wardroom mess and I had a few minutes talk with him. Their steamers Alliance and Brigham are waiting a week or so for some riverboats to be finished, which they will tow up.

Tuesday, June 28. 2 P.M.

This morning we passed two sailing vessels bound north. The only sail we have seen since leaving Onualaska. We are now somewhere about N. of Cape Smith, nearly N62degrees and W168 or 169 degrees. No land in sight.

It seems pretty cold. There has been no rain since morning but it is cloudy. The sea is remarkably quiet today but VanWyck has taken to his bed again. There are nine fellows of the ships crew sick. Four or five of them have the mumps.

It is five o'clock at Fools Paradise and I can see somebody starting a fire and getting supper. I am hoping that I will hear from you soon after I reach St. M. Possibly mail may not come very often in which case I'll not get many letters, so make them <u>big</u> ones.

<u>Wednesday 6/29</u>. This morning when we went on deck the wind was blowing fresh from the east . . . the land . . . and it was very much warmer than it has been for the last two days. Last night we were in sight of St. Lawrence Island and saw two ships in the distance. The sun set at 10:15 and was a gorgeous sight. This morning a few points of high land on the N. side of Norton Sound were in sight. The color of the water has changed from bluish green to brown showing us that we were going thru the Yukon's waters. This plainly marked current sets off to the N.W. toward Behring Straits. Out here many miles from the river's mouth we saw a lot of pieces of drift.

3:00 P.M. While you are eating supper I will write a little more. The wind has gone down and it is warm and comfortable. The temperature of the water is frequently taken and John is having samples of the water taken in bottles to test the density of it. This shows how the water of the Yukon affects the Sea. The water today is very much warmer than yesterday, which must account for the more comfortable weather than it was at 38 degrees. Now it is 57 degrees.

This forenoon we passed two full-rigged ships, one, the "Elwell" signaled her name and the Wheeling responded. A ship at sea with all sails set is a handsome object and shows to best effect from another vessel. It seemed like shaking hands with someone.

By lunchtime we were thru the brown stained waters of the Yukon and in sight of Cape Darby north of St. Michael. We will reach our destination some time tonight. (Farther North 64 degrees 17 feet)

St. Michael, June 30.

We reached here at 10 last night and found the "Bear." St. Paul and Roanoke were in the harbor, also seven schooners and several riverboats. A small fleet of rowboats and canoes came around, several people asking about steamers coming with boat in tow. An officer in full dress from the Bear came aboard with the compliments of the Capt. of the Bear to Capt. Subree. This morning a Lieutenant came over from the Wheeling conveying Capt.

Subree's compliments to the Capt. of the Bear, followed by a call from the Capt. of the Bear. Then Capt. Subree, in full dress, goes off to call on the Commandant at the Army Post.

John and one of the men from our ship went ashore this morning to see about a camping place, but have not yet returned. Our boats, eight of them, and some of the Wheeling's boats have been loaded with our effects and are on their way to land. We will get dinner on board tonight but will have camp up and sleep ashore. The Nelson with the launches has not yet arrived, but we can begin work here with small boats. VanWyck seems very ill. He will have to be moved to a house ashore and be taken care of.

<u>July 1st.</u> We pitched our camp yesterday and have things as comfortable as possible under the circumstances. The tents are all small, just large enough for two. Mr. Faris and I occupy one. We each have a cot, mattress, pillow and sheet and two blankets. We have mosquito bars over the beds, without which it would be impossible to sleep with any comfort. There are swarms of mosquitos. There is a village about a mile from here near the entrance to the bay. Dr. Edmonds was here thru the winter of 1891, so he found several acquaintances among the natives. Now they live in tents made of cotton cloth very much as the Siwashes of the Sound do, but in winter they have houses (?) made of logs and rubbish covered with sod.

At one place I saw a pipe made of walrus tusk, remarkably well carved. On the sides were hunting scenes, natives dancing, etc. The old chap was only asking $20.for it, so I didn't get it.

In one of their places a common meetinghouse, where they have their dances, etc. we were much interested. The entrance was thru an anteroom with a door 2 X 2 1/2 ft. at the back end. You crawl thru and are ready to dance. In very cold weather you go down thru the floor of the anteroom, crawl along underneath and come up thru the floor inside. But I must turn in if I get up at 3:30. Will tell you the rest next time.

Love to you all,
George

Chapter Fifteen

*T*he surveying of the Bering Sea area took many weeks, the one consolation for Hazen was that he could see his brother John Francis who was commander of the Coast and Geodetic Survey steamer Patterson in Alaskan waters from 1809 through 1904.

Commander John Francis Pratt

Coast and Geodetic Survey Party

George Hazen Pratt second from left.
John Francis Pratt fourth from right.

However, Hazen was back in Seattle when the time for the birth of the new baby was near.

"I'm going to be here with you this time, Emma. Absolutely," he told his wife.

When Emma felt the first labor pains his apparent ease turned into the nervousness and worry of every man about to become a father. This time it was a little baby boy. It was with great pleasure they approached the universal problem of what in the world to name this new little person.

"I love your name." Emma looked directly into Hazen's eyes.

"But we can't have two 'boys' named George Hazen." Hazen grinned at Emma, but Emma was serious.

"Let's at least use Hazen as part of his name . . . please," she begged.

Hazen pondered. "What can we put with that?"

Suddenly his face lit up.

"We've used a Pratt name, so why not put a Clarke name with it? Your papa, Emma. Your papa's name . . . Thomas. Wouldn't Thomas Hazen Pratt sound just right together?"

"Oh my, you have come up with a great idea! I love it. Thomas Hazen is just perfect. Papa will be so happy when he hears the news." She reached up to Hazen who was now standing by her bedside. He bent down to kiss her upturned face.

"I love you, Emma Clarke Pratt. It was the happiest day of my life the day I met you."

"And I can say the same, my dear. We are two of the most fortunate people in the world to have found each other."

A young Thomas Hazen Pratt

Emma was busy indeed after that, with looking after Fool's Paradise besides taking care of their two children.

When Hazen's surveying of the Alaska area was finished soon after 1900 he was again in Seattle with his family. It was fine and they were happy to be together, but Hazen did not have work. He spent days searching the Seattle area for work. They were finishing breakfast one morning when Hazen sighed,

"Well, Polly, I am at a loss. There is no work here in Seattle."

"I know, dear. I've been thinking about it quite a lot. I wonder if you had thought of your brother Will . . . who is in Illinois now, isn't he?"

"Will? Hmmmm..... Yes, he works for U. S. Steel there. What could a surveyor do for them in Illinois?"

"George Hazen Pratt! You can do anything you put your mind to. You know that. Why not see if Will would have a job you could do there?"

"And leave our beloved state of Washington?"

"If necessary . . . for the time being . . . yes."

Hazen wrote Will.

Will wrote back saying that he would be able to come up with something for Hazen by the time they could get to Illinois.

William Henry Pratt . . . another of George Hazen's brothers ready to help him. What would he do without his brothers? Arthur stood up with him when he married Emma. John Francis helped him get work surveying the Yukon, and now Will was going to come up with a job for him when he was out of work. Brothers for Hazen had proved to be his best friends.

There was a general scurrying around to get ready to leave. Farewell parties with their friends, renting their little house, working it out with Nelson to care for Fool's Paradise, and convincing the children it was going to be an adventure going on the train to Illinois.

The children were easily convinced. They were looking forward to going. Neither of them had ever been on a train before. They were happy looking out the windows of the train, going to eat in the dining car and with just the general idea of traveling to another part of the country. However, their happy feelings turned to fright when they came to the peak of the mountains in northern Idaho. Hazen was telling them about the pass coming up where the elevation was over 3,000 feet.

"But still, Daddy, it's beautiful . . . even if it's a little scary," Dorothy said.

"We're safe here in the train, Dot. Nothing to be afraid of."

No sooner were the words out of Hazen's mouth than the train was brought to an unexpected and rapid halt.

"What's the matter, Daddy?" Thomas crawled up onto Hazen's lap.

"Well, I don't know just now. There's some smoke coming from up near the head of the train. Let's take a look outside." Carrying Thomas on his arm Hazen headed for the door of their car on the train. Emma took Dorothy by the hand and followed along, curious too, about why they had stopped. The smoke that billowed out from the front of the train was not from the train, but was from the wooden trestle bridge that crossed over 4th of July Pass. Some of the other passengers joined them outside and all were astounded to see the wooden bridge itself on fire.

"Daddy! The bridge we're supposed to cross over is on fire!" Dorothy was clutching at her papa's jacket edge anxiously.

"So it is, Dot. So it is."

Almost immediately the train engineer was outside the train calling out to the disembarked passengers.

"Please stay on the train, people, until we figure out what to do here. Please. Get back on the train."

"Come on, children. Get up these steps and onto the train. We wouldn't want to be left behind if the train started backing up, would we?"

Hazen was laughing at them as they climbed up the steps. They all went back to their seats and sat down, waiting for what would happen next.

"Papa, were those people by the bridge Indians? They looked like the pictures I've seen of Indians." Dorothy asked earnestly.

"Yes, Dot, they looked like Indians to me, too."

"Did they set fire to the bridge, Papa?"

Hazen hesitated. "I'm not sure, but it looked as if they might have. I think we'll have to ask the engineer or the conductor when we see them."

Before very long the engineer and the conductor were both hurrying through the car trying to reassure the passengers that everything would be alright. They couldn't stop them for questioning then.

At last the announcement was made to everyone, one car at a time, that they were going to all get off the train and walk down the side of the canyon and climb back up again on the other side.

"Please, Mr. Conductor, can you tell us who set fire to the bridge? Was it those people we thought were Indians?" Dorothy had her hand on the conductor's sleeve.

The conductor looked at Dorothy, glanced up at Hazen and after Hazen's nod he answered her.

"Yes, we are pretty sure it was those Indians who set fire to the bridge. We still have no idea why they would do it. They left so fast we couldn't question them. But . . . they're gone now and there is no need to worry about them when you go down the canyon." He patted Dorothy's hand, smiling at her.

The conductor insisted there would be another train waiting for them by the time they had made it up the other side of the pass.

After all the fear and anxiety that had been overwhelming them the children began jumping up and down with excitement now. The train ride was turning out to be a true adventure.

The descent down the steep-sided canyon was treacherous for some, but Hazen, Emma and the children were able to do it in the spirit of a fun activity . . . more like a game than a thing they were forced to do.

"Hold my hand, Dorothy," Emma called. "I need your help to keep from slipping."

"I'll help you, Mama." Dorothy, proud to be needed by her mother, grasped Emma's hand.

Hazen wound up carrying Thomas, grasping tree roots and tufts of grass as they nearly slid all the way down. While they were sliding Dorothy thought of something no one else had.

"What about our luggage, Papa? Shouldn't we be bringing that with us?"

"The conductor told me they would bring everyone's luggage later. Let's hope it won't be so much later it doesn't get on this other train. We will just have to trust them . . ."

Climbing up the other side of the steep canyon was more work than going down had been. Hazen was concerned about Emma and Dorothy.

"Emma, why don't you let me help Dot and you can bring Thomas. I don't think either of them can manage by themselves."

Before they could go any further he came up with a better idea.

"Dot, where is the jump rope you had before we started down the other side?"

"Right here, Papa. Didn't you see me tie it around my middle?"

She struggled with the rope to untie it, finally able to hand it to him.

"There, Papa. What are you going to do with it?"

"I'm going to use it to help us get up this steep canyon."

While Dorothy had been untying the jump rope from her waist he had been removing his leather belt from his trousers. He looped the belt around little Thomas's midsection, took out his jackknife and punched a new hole in the belt and then refastened it around Thomas so that it fit snugly.

Hazen turned to Emma.

"Can you hang onto this and pull Thomas up the incline with yourself? He can walk some when on his feet and that will help."

"Of course, I can tug this little guy along with me, but . . ."

"But what?"

"Who's going to tug me?"

Emma began laughing and soon all four of them were laughing. Even Thomas laughed because the others did even though he didn't understand.

"All right now," Hazen stopped laughing, then smiled at Emma and began to explain to his family.

"This jump rope is for all of us to grip and hold onto tight. Do you understand? I will be first and pull you along. You each need to help by climbing as much and as best you can. We will be our own little train."

While the Pratt family had been talking and making preparations part of the other passengers had climbed the canyon. Some were still climbing and unbelievably to Hazen, another train had indeed appeared at the top of the canyon.

"I can see the other train up there. Come on, team, let's climb this canyon!"

Hazen started up the side of the canyon. He was delighted that his little family had paid heed to his admonitions and were all really climbing. He could hardly feel any drag on the jump rope in his hand. Dorothy followed her papa, then Emma with one hand on the jump rope and the other gripping the belt that encircled young Thomas Hazen.

"Toot-toot, Papa! We're climbing! We're nearly at the top!" Dorothy was short of breath and puffing, but playing the game.

The last passengers that had not boarded the new train were watching the Pratts all tied together and climbing. When Hazen, Emma and the children reached the top the waiting passengers cheered and clapped. Emma was embarrassed but secretly proud of the way Hazen had organized them for the tough climb.

They all boarded the train exhausted and happy to sit down for the rest of their trip.

"Papa, do you think there will be a dining car on this train?" Dorothy asked immediately.

"Worked up an appetite, did you? Well, I sincerely hope there's a dining car. I'm pretty hungry myself."

Hazen grinned at her. "Shall we ask the conductor?"

Chapter Sixteen

The little incident on the train trip from Seattle to Illinois was burned into Dorothy's young mind. It was something she never forgot and she frequently told the story of it in later years to her grandchildren. The years following this adventure were extremely calm in comparison.

The family lived with Will in his house in Evanston for the first months in the mid-west, then a bit later moved to Rogers Park on the north side of Chicago. The children made friends with other children in the neighborhood as well as those in school. Dorothy had been enrolled in school, made friends and seemed happy. In the summers she was sent to Vermont to visit and stay with the Pratt relatives. She thoroughly enjoyed Vermont and it made a deep impression on her. While in Vermont she began drawing. When she returned to Illinois one fall she surprised Emma and Hazen by carrying a portfolio under her arm.

"What do you have there, dear, under your arm?" Emma asked. Hazen looked at her to see what she was going to say.

"I started drawing pictures of what I saw in Vermont. Wait 'til you see, Papa! You might recognize some of my pictures. At least, I hope you can," she laughed.

Both parents were eager to get home and see Dorothy's portfolio and she was eager to show off her work of the summer.

At home, after examining the number of drawings Dorothy had made of familiar scenes of Vermont . . . familiar at least to Hazen . . . he looked up at Emma, who met his surprised look with one of her own. Dorothy's work was amazing. It was so realistic that Hazen recognized every scene she had drawn.

"These look just like the real thing, Dot. You've done very well indeed. I'm impressed," Hazen said as he put his arm around his daughter's shoulders.

"They are beautiful, Dorothy. They make me want to leave for Vermont right away." Emma joined in with praise.

Dorothy basked in their words for a bit then dashed out of the house to go find her friends she had sorely missed while she was away.

"Well, Emma, what do you think of all this?" Hazen asked.

"Like you, Mr. Pratt, I am impressed. Still more, I am totally surprised. I had no idea she had artistic talent."

"Nor I." Hazen said thoughtfully.

They were both quiet for a few moments then turned toward each other, both with the same thought.

"We must do something about this talent, Emma."

"I am in total agreement. What can we do?"

"Do you know of any special art school where we could send her?"

"Truthfully, no, but I will talk to my friends and look in the school directories. We'll find one, Mr. Pratt. We will find one for her."

They did. Very shortly Dorothy was enrolled for classes at the Evanston Art Academy, which proved to be not far from where they were living on Lunt Avenue in Rogers Park.

Dot and Emma looking at Dot's drawings

Dorothy was delighted with the school where she made many new friends . . . all of whom were talented young people in the artistic world. When she brought home some of her notebooks Emma noticed the wide margins and here and there among her schoolwork writings were little drawings of birds or flowers and once in awhile a small sketch of a fellow student or one of the teachers. Besides artwork there were classes in Math and Science as well as English and Drawing.

This is one of Dot's little drawings, done in 1910 when she was fifteen.

Emma secretly wondered about the little drawings and whether her daughter was paying attention in the classes not related to art. She, however, never mentioned it to Hazen as she knew he would chastise Dorothy, perhaps even severely, which might spoil the whole concept of an education in art for her daughter. Dorothy's report card quieted their worries.

CHICAGO ACADEMY OF FINE ARTS, 81 East Madison Street, CHICAGO
REPORT OF **Miss Dorothy Pratt,** FOR MONTH OF **MARCH 1915,**
SENT TO **Mr. C. H. Pratt, No. 2119 Lunt Ave., Chicago, Ill.**

The Pratts looked around for a church to attend when they moved to the north side of Chicago. They finally decided on the Rogers Park Baptist Church. Dorothy went with them, of course, and after Church she went to the Sunday School Class for her age group.

James Paul Randell, son of one of their neighbors, was in the same Sunday School Class and he and Dorothy became good friends. The two families had met so the Pratts weren't surprised or concerned with the amount of time the two young people spent together. The days and years sped by. Soon it was graduation time for Dorothy as well as James Randell. Neither the Randells or the Pratts realized it, but by now Dorothy and James had become quite smitten with each other.

One evening soon after graduation Dorothy came to talk to Emma.

"Mama, James has asked me to marry him."

Emma was busy in the kitchen and had her back toward Dorothy when Dorothy told her this startling bit of news, so the shock on her face was not visible to her daughter.

"You're both a bit young to be thinking of marriage, aren't you?" she asked.

"How old were you when you married, Mama?"

"I was twenty-four and Papa was thirty-three."

"You were almost an old maid, Mama."

"Dorothy Pratt! What an unkind thing to say! I was definitely not an old maid. I went on to college and got my teaching credential."

"Well, a lot of girls my age are getting married. Mama, we're in love! We want to spend the rest of our lives together! Please speak to Papa before I tell him that James is coming to ask him if he can have his blessing for us to get married."

"I'll speak to Papa."

Speaking to Hazen was just as Emma had known it would be. Dorothy had been wise to speak to her mother first.

"When did our darling daughter give you this bit of information?" he asked testily. "Marry at eighteen? What is she thinking of?"

Hazen had been reading the paper. Now he put the paper down, stood up, looked at Emma meaningfully. It was as if he was about to go out and find the two young people immediately. He stood for a few moments, shook his head and then began the pacing she was so familiar with. Given a major problem, Hazen paced the floor. This, without a doubt, was a problem . . . for both of them.

"Do you know anything about this Randell kid?" Hazen asked.

"As much as you do. The family, we know, lives just down the street and they go to the same church we do. I think that is where they became so well acquainted . . . the children, I mean . . . in Sunday School Class."

Emma was torn. She understood her daughter and at the same time, she understood Hazen. What should they do? They discussed, argued and pondered, both winding up thinking the same thing. The two young people should wait.

When Emma and Hazen told Dorothy their decision she stormed out of the house. Needless to say, the family was being sorely tested.

Dorothy and James compared notes. Dorothy found that the Randell parents hadn't been any more pleased with their ideas than the Pratts had been.

"What can we do, James? Neither your folks nor mine will give us their blessing."

"I can't understand them at all. We may have to do it on our own."

"On our own? What do you mean?"

"We could just go ahead and do it."

Dorothy looked embarrassed.

"You mean . . . just go ahead and . . . get married?"

"Yes. Go ahead and get married."

"But how can we do that without their approval? We're underage."

"Let me think on it." James walked up and down along the pathway in the park where they had met to talk things over. Dorothy sat on a nearby bench as he walked. Finally, he yelled, "I've got it!" Dorothy jumped up and ran toward him.

"What? What? Tell me!"

James was grinning.

"We just need to have the approval of an adult, right?"

"I think so."

"Well . . . let's find Aunt Belle."

"Aunt Belle?"

"Yes. She likes us and thinks it's okay for us to get married."

"That's true, she does. Oh yes, she does! I'm so glad you thought of her, Jim!"

The two young people were desperate to be married . . . to be together. However . . . before they could carry out any plan at all Emma and Hazen purchased a railroad ticket for Dorothy to go to Florida to spend the winter with her Uncle. The young people didn't have any time at all to carry out James' plan. Emma kept her daughter so fully occupied choosing clothes, packing up and getting ready to go she didn't even get to say goodbye to James. Dorothy did write to James as soon as she arrived in Florida explaining what had happened, that she had been kidnapped and rushed off to Florida. The unhappy young people continued their romance by the U.S. Mail. They plotted and dreamed and came up with a new plan.

For carrying out his plan James enlisted the help of Aunt Belle, who lived with the Randell family. James was right. Aunt Belle was sympathetic toward the young couple and she agreed to go up to Muskegon with James when he made a trip to Michigan. The trip was, ostensibly, to check out a piece of real estate in Muskegon. Which he did . . . taking Aunt Belle with him to "keep me company," he told his parents.

After a day in Muskegon of work for his father James was ready to launch his plan.

"Well, Aunt Belle, we've taken care of the little job for my dad. Now we can get down to the real purpose of this trip," James grinned at his aunt.

Belle smiled back at him with the same knowing look.

"All right, but you'll have to explain to me what to do, James. You are here and Dorothy is in Florida. How is that going to work?"

James just kept grinning at her.

"If we wait one more day I think you'll find the answer, Aunt Belle."

Sure enough, the next day James took his Aunt to the station to meet the train from Chicago and who should step off but a radiant young Dorothy Pratt. She had made the switch at the station in Chicago and instead of getting off the train from Florida had transferred to another train headed north to Muskegon. The two had planned well.

James found a Baptist Minister who was willing to perform the ceremony for them. James had also made sure they had the papers needed before and after the ceremony. They could take them back to Chicago as proof to both families they were legally married on September 29, 1915. Legally married in spite of all objections. Belle was a willing witness to the ceremony.

James rented two rooms in a hotel in Muskegon for the three of them. Belle graciously found something else to do and somewhere else to spend the evening, leaving the newlyweds on their own.

When the three returned to Chicago the next day it was to be greeted by complete silence in the Randell household along with disapproving looks at Belle for supporting James and Dorothy.

At the Pratt household Emma looked across the room at Hazen who was no longer pacing the floor. It was far too late for that. Their "little girl" was married . . . without their approval.

Hazen returned Emma's look, "Well, I guess we have a real independent child."

"Yes. It's a done thing. We will have to change our ideas and accept that our daughter is now a married woman and . . . accept James as our son-in-law. We can't let this be the thing that has us cutting our daughter out of our lives," Emma said.

"I agree. Hard as it is to do, I agree." Hazen said sadly.

The two families agreed on one point. It was done. They all joined, somewhat reluctantly, in giving the couple belated congratulations and in making formal announcements of the marriage.

Emma and Hazen were completely surprised to learn that young James had found a home for the couple. The two were soon shopping for furniture for it.

"I'll have to give him credit, James is providing for Dot . . . in a manner neither you nor I can find any fault with," Hazen admitted to Emma a few months after the wedding.

"True. Plus, Mr. Pratt, they do seem really happy together. I think we will have to give our belated . . . and genuine . . . approval of the marriage. I guess it is just that to us they seem so young."

"Too young . . . far too young." Hazen said.

Chapter Seventeen

*T*he months sped by. Dorothy and James started a family very soon after settling into their new little house. Emma and Hazen were not too surprised when one day their daughter quietly whispered to her mother, "Guess what, Mama? We're going to have a baby! And you and Papa will be Grandma and Grandpa!"

On December 6th Dorothy went into labor. The baby was a little boy, which seemed to delight everyone.

"What will you name this little fellow?" Emma asked Dorothy.

"James, Jr., of course, Mama," Dorothy looked up shyly from her hospital bed. "Does it sound all right to have his middle name Pratt?"

Emma and Hazen smiled at their daughter.

"Of course it is," they answered . . . practically in unison.

Both sets of grandparents and James' sister Isabelle doted on the new little boy. He was almost a year old when Dorothy confided in her mama that she thought she was pregnant again. Fortunately, with all the members of the family close by there was never a problem of not having someone to look after young James, who was by now being called Jimmy.

Jimmy wasn't even two in 1918 when the second little boy was born. It didn't take long to come up with a name for him.

"After all, Mama, Jimmy was a name from the Randell family. We think this little boy should be named from the Pratt family."

Here Dorothy paused.

"We thought George was a nice name."

Of course Hazen and Emma were delighted that the couple had chosen George Hazen's first name.

"And the middle name this time?" Emma asked.

"Turn about is fair play, right?'

Emma nodded.

"How does George Milton sound?"

"Perfect."

The young couple seemed to be doing a very good job of keeping the members of both families happy.

Dorothy didn't recover quite as well from this birth. She was exhausted and listless most of the time afterward. Emma and Hazen engaged a special doctor for her. Nothing seemed to help, even a trip up to Muskegon, Michigan to check property again while the rest of the family cared for the two little boys in order to give Dorothy a break. The family was jolted to learn that soon after the trip to Muskegon Dorothy once again found herself pregnant.

Amazingly, Dorothy's state of health improved during this pregnancy and the family began all looking forward to the possibility that this time it might be a little girl. Not to be. On April 28th, 1920 another little boy arrived.

"And what will this little one be named, Dorothy?" Emma asked.

"We've decided on Edward, Mama. Edward William. Edward comes from your grandfather, Mama . . . Edward Dowling Clarke . . . and William is for Uncle Will." She looked up at her papa. "I hope he'll like it."

"Edward William sounds fine to me, dear. You've chosen names that are just right." Emma smiled openly. Hazen gave her a big smile, too. He was still amazed that his very own Dot was mothering three boys. He remembered his own boyhood. There were four boys then with Lizzie coming in as number five.

1919

Dorothy and James were busy parents with three little guys. Lots of help came from both families. It was in early 1922 that Dorothy became pregnant once again.

"We're going to be lucky, Mama. This time it will be a little girl."

Emma just smiled.

It wasn't a little girl. Once more it was a boy. It took quite awhile to come up with a name, which turned out to be John.

"John. Middle name this time, Dot?" Hazen asked.

"We thought John Rogers . . . John is for Papa's brother John Francis and the Rogers is James's grandmother's maiden name. John Rogers Randell sounds nice, doesn't it?" Dorothy smiled as she cradled her newborn son.

While Emma and Hazen lived in Illinois Hazen's father Joseph Henry Pratt came for a prolonged visit with them. While there he wrote back to cousins in Vermont in his particular spidery handwriting.

604 Estes Ave., Chicago, Ill.
March 27, 1905

Dear Cousins Alice and Willis,
I send you a letter that I received from cousin Benjamin Dutton some days ago thinking you would like to hear from him.

As for myself I am staying with George and Emma. They take good care of me. Emma is a remarkable woman, always pleasant and happy and keeps the whole family in good order. She takes me around the city about once a week . . . by the way, this is a mighty city. Almost two million inhabitants. Every thing here is done on a big scale and the railroad traffick is enormous compared with Vermont.

Will and George are very busy at the steel works now. George has charge of one building, which makes all kinds of paints. He leaves home in the morning at half past six and gets back at the same time at night. It is some 8 miles to the works. They go and come in the cars. We had about one foot of snow here in February but it is all gone now. I think the Season is about one month earlier than in Vermont.

Emma and I went to the funeral yesterday of a Mr. Smith who was a great friend of O. M. Tinkham and the same age. Born in 1831. The funeral was in Covenant Church on Halsted Street.

I have had two sick spells since I came here but am on my feet now. Don't know but I am wearing out doing nothing.

Love to all,
J. H. Pratt

Chapter Eighteen

A year later, in 1923, it was time for Hazen to retire from U.S. Steel, where he had been working with brother Will.

"Well, Emma . . . ."

Emma looked up at her husband. She stood up and threw her arms around him in a tremendous hug.

"Yes, Mr. Pratt! Yes! I'm ready!"

Hazen just grinned. She knew. He held her close dancing and twirling her around the room.

They were going home . . . home to that glorious place in the far West known as the Washington Territory. Their most favorite place in all of the whole wide world. Going home.

Even the news that their daughter Dorothy was once again pregnant did not deter them from their decision to head west . . . west to Washington. They added figures, checked the stock purchases Hazen had made while working for U.S. Steel, added those figures to his retirement from the steel company and felt they could live comfortably. They bought their train tickets, packed their meager belongings and headed for home.

Dorothy could hardly believe her parents would leave to go so far away from her when she was expecting another child. If truth were known she was deeply hurt by their decision, but she kept it to herself. When her delivery time drew near she was still feeling hurt to be without her parents. But when the baby was born and it turned out to be the little girl they had been hoping for, hoping for so many times, all her sad feelings vanished and she and James were supremely happy. James's parents and his sister Isabelle all pitched in to help care for the four boys while Dorothy recovered from the birth.

"At last we have our little girl," Dorothy smiled widely at James.

"Yup, we do. Finally. What are we going to name her?" he asked. Before she could answer he continued, "I vote for Dorothy. How about Dorothy Isabelle? That sounds mighty good to me."

He grinned at his wife.

"But what would we call her? Two Dorothys might be confusing, don't you think?"

"We could call her Dotty . . . how about calling her Dotty? I like that."

Dorothy couldn't resist his enthusiasm. "All right. Dorothy it is . . . and Dotty for short."

Emma and Hazen were delighted to hear the news from Chicago that their newest grandchild was at last a girl.

"Oh, how happy they must be to have a little girl at long last," Emma said.

"Maybe we brought them good luck by leaving the area," Hazen quipped.

Emma gave him a sharp look.

"Just trying to make a joke, Emma . . . just a joke . . . really."

The two of them were so happy to be back in Washington Territory nothing could have spoiled it for them. They had their small house in Kirkland and were busy with working in the yard and establishing a new garden.

One morning at the breakfast table Emma poured Hazen a second cup of coffee while he was reading the morning paper.

"Are you having any second thoughts, Mr. Pratt?" she asked.

Hazen peered over his paper.

"Second thoughts about what, love?"

"Second thoughts about our coming all the way out here to Washington and leaving our Dorothy back in Chicago."

"No second thoughts as long as my sweet Emma is here pouring me another cup of coffee every morning," Hazen grinned at her, put down the paper and reached across the table for Emma's hand pulling her up and toward him. She wound up stumbling around the table and falling onto Hazen's lap, which was just exactly what he had intended. His arms were around her holding her close as he kissed her.

"No second thoughts, Emma, no second thoughts. I'm still in love with you. Maybe even more so."

"More so than what?" Emma turned her head so he couldn't see her teasing smile.

"More so than I ever have, love. The way I feel about you still overwhelms me. Just like it did all those years ago when I rowed across the sound to see you."

"And I thought you were just coming into Papa's store for supplies."

"Only that first time. After I met you it was never just for supplies. It was to see if your papa would ask me home for supper one more time."

"I guess he did, too. Sometimes when I was teaching on the Island I wasn't there."

"But one time you were. Remember the porch swing?"

"How could I forget, Mr. Pratt? It was the very beginning of life for me. The very beginning." Emma laid her head on Hazen's shoulder as he held her ever closer. "I am so happy you asked that question, Mr. Pratt. Do you remember how quickly I said yes?"

He nuzzled her neck. "I do."

Chapter Nineteen

Should we sell Fools Paradise, Mr. Pratt?"
Emma asked Hazen one morning as she watched
him cultivating the little garden he had planted in
the back yard.

"Why don't you hang onto it for a while longer?
It makes a great getaway place for us for a change
of scene now and then," Hazen said. "Besides, we
can't plant enough here to dry or can and preserve
for our food supply . . . can we?"

"Probably not. I hadn't thought of it that way."

Then teasingly she said, "If we sold Fool's
Paradise you would have to come up with another
way to get in a good day of fishing."

Emma looking at one of Hazen's catches of the day.

"Which I probably might be able to do," Hazen laughed. "That is . . . if I had to."

He grinned as he toppled a dirt clod over in her path in the garden. She laughed and flipped the clod back to him with her toe.

Later that evening Hazen leaned back in his chair after eating a fish dinner perfectly prepared by Emma. It was a dinner from the fish he had caught that day while out with his friend Whittenmeyer.

"Mama, no one else in the world can prepare fish as well as you do. No one else can do them justice. That was the best fish dinner I've ever eaten. Absolutely."

One morning in early January as they sat at the breakfast table lingering over a second cup of coffee, Emma said, "Mr. Pratt, we must be thinking of something to send our Dorothy for her birthday . . . and Tom's too."

"Yes, I know. I was thinking the same thing. How about our going into Seattle to do a little shopping?"

"Good idea. Do you have any thoughts as to what they might like, Mr. Pratt?"

"Well, we can send Tom money as usual. That seems to please him the most. As for our Dorothy, let's try Friedlander's. Maybe we'll get an idea there."

"Friedlander's is a jewelry store, Mr. Pratt. Were you thinking of jewelry for our Dorothy?"

"Don't they sell silverware there, too?"

"Silverware. That does sound like a good idea. If I hurry I can be ready soon."

Emma cleared away their breakfast remains and hurried into the bedroom to change into her 'going to Seattle' clothes.

FERRY   KIRKLAND WASH

They took the ferry to Seattle and soon found Friedlander's. They wound up selecting a dozen sterling silver teaspoons in a simple, plain design.

"We'd like these initialed if that is possible," Hazen said.

"Certainly, sir," the clerk replied.

Hazen turned to Emma. "How about DPR, Emma . . . use all three initials? We can't leave the Pratt out can we?"

"Absolutely not, Mr. Pratt. DPR is perfect."

The clerk wrote up the order with Dorothy's Michigan address and told them the silver would be sent out directly to Dorothy Pratt Randell when the engraving was finished. Hazen paid and they were soon on their way back across the sound to Kirkland.

Hazen turned to Emma as they sat together on the ferry. He put his arm around her shoulders and squeezed her with a smile.

"Good deed, well done."

"Yes, indeed, Mr. Pratt. I love shopping with you. No waffling about whatsoever."

Hazen grinned. "Now to mail a check to Tom and we're finished for another year."

It still amazed Emma and Hazen that both of their children should be born on the same date . . . January 11ᵗʰ . . . just different years. On the morning of the 11ᵗʰ Hazen made note in his diary.

'This is the children's birthday. We wonder if Dot has the twelve teaspoons we sent her and if she's pleased with them, if Tom got the money and what he did with it.'

Later, in March he penned a long letter to his daughter. Dot had evidently written them to thank them . . . perhaps she had written several times before Hazen sat down with his pen to write a long letter to thank her for remembering his birthday on March first.

Kirkland, March 5ᵗʰ

Dear Dot._

Your good letter and handsome necktie came on the minute for my birthday. I feel a keen appreciation of your thoughtfulness in remembering the day, for your letters _ as usual with your letters _ are our chief source of satisfaction and comfort outside of our own efforts.

We are glad to hear about the children _ Jack seems to have started kindergarten under a full head of steam wanting two sessions a day. His good-looking head will be filled with schoolwork as fast as it is handed out to him. I think the teacher should have sent you a note when she changed Bud. Sometimes, when you know what the difficulty is, a little help and encouragement from Mother makes a difference. Eddie's valentines are neatly done. Tell him "Thank you." We like them very much.

We were much interested in your Washington's Birthday observance. It surely was a great treat. We, too, heard the President's address at our next-door neighbors. Seems quite wonderful that we were listening with you to the same voice at the same time. We have also heard two operas by radio _ Carmen and Il Travatore _ Seattle Civic Opera Ass'n.

We have noticed in the daily weather report that you seemed to be having a mild winter for Chicago, but your roses had better not get too ambitious. Our winter has been mild and the temperature often goes to 50 degrees in the warmest part of the day, but there seems to be some quality of the air lacking, which goes with real spring. So far only one daffodil is in full blossom, while last year there were many of all kinds. Also an apricot tree was in full bloom on the 7th. I had potatoes and peas planted on March 1st last year and had to cut the grass in February. But this year the most of the ground has been too wet from the frequent rains. Have just got a big load of fertilizer, which I will try to spade under during the coming week.

On this narrow lot there isn't much room, so our vegetable garden and a good part of our berry bushes are on adjoining lots, a part of which I have cleared of brush and stumps and fertilized. Climbing roses against the house didn't do well so this winter I cleared and dug up a piece 8X35 north of our front yard. Have set a tall post at each end, guyed with wire to keep them plumb and have stretched wire netting between them. It is nine ft. high and we called it our billboard, but after it gets covered with roses we think it will be all right.

Mrs. Whittenmeyer is something of an authority on birds of this section. She was asked to give a talk to the Woman's Club of Monroe on the 24th and they asked us to go too. We left Mamma and Mrs. W. at a lady's house where they had lunch as a preliminary to the gathering, while W. and I kept on up the Skykomish River to Startup (look at your map) where we cooked our coffee & bacon and eggs _ somewhat dubious about encountering that big houseful of ladies at Monroe. Then came back to Sultan and went up the Sultan River, crossing it about three miles above the village and going on up the west side. The present road evidently is appropriating the bed of what is shown on your topographical map to be a logging railroad. At a place where the river makes a sharp bend, locally called the "horseshoe" a fence and locked gate bear notice that beyond lay the watershed of the City of Everett, and forbidding trespass. We had been following the pipeline for a few miles and hoped we could keep on to the intake. But there we could look down into the canyon to the greenish tinted water some 300 feet below. The river enters the canyon below the Sultan Basin away to the northeast and remains in this almost inaccessible gorge until within about a mile and a half of the bridge. In places the steep slope can be climbed, but no great distance along the stream can be traversed before cliffs rising from the water stop further progress.

At Monroe we waited a few minutes for the end of that bird talk and came home.

Sunday March 6th

The brown lines on the topographical sheets are contour lines showing the shape and height of hills and mountains. On the one called "Sultan Quadrangle" (name in upper right corner) the space between them represents 100 ft. in elevation and is called the contour interval. (See bottom of sheet) Every 500 or 1000 feet (in elevation) the line is made heavier and somewhere along it you will find its elevation marked in figures.

So you see that to the east of us there is much very rugged mountainous country.

Our love,
Dad

Hazen tucked a photo into his letter. It was of Emma and himself with their very good friends the Whittenmeyers. The two couples spent much time together and one could see their happiness in the photo he sent.

Chapter Twenty

*A*s the years sped on Emma and Hazen's activities slowed in similar cadence. Emma was able to keep up with her group meetings but Hazen slowed visibly. He found it most difficult to give up his fishing expeditions. One April Emma wrote to Dorothy from, surprisingly, the hospital . . .

My dear Dorothy___
Your welcome letters have reached me promptly. Send no more to the Hospital. Will be back home in a few days and Papa can have the pleasure of getting them at the Post Office.
Am going to Carolyn's for a few days because she is so insistent and to be near the Doctor in case anything goes wrong.

This was a <u>uterine</u> operation entirely. The bladder has been sewed in place supported by the uterus and stitches taken where they will do the most good, so it is waiting for them to heal which caused me to stay so long in the hospital, where I have very good care and food.

Carolyn Steele has certainly acted heroic in cleaning our house for us. Her husband has Kalsomined the ceilings of the Dining and Living rooms right over the wall paper, which was quite smokey and soiled when we moved in a year and a half ago. Also they have Kalsomined the whole of Papa's bedroom, <u>cream</u> as it was before and much in need of it, being off the Dining room where the stove is. The bathroom between our bedrooms is deep cream also and my bedroom, where the homemade dressing table is, I believe has light gray walls and cream ceiling. She even took off the covers of the dressing table and washed them. The whole house was quite clean before they began but now it must be quite sanitary and "spick and span." Of course we are paying them a nominal amount for their trouble but no amount of money will pay for all the things they have done for us.

The weather has been cool and rainy nearly ever since I came here so there has been no gardening time. Poor Daddy has been so distressed about my operation and about the cleaning going on in the house but he is much relieved now it is over and will be quite happy when I get back. Our friend Mrs. Whittenmeyer has had him to noon dinner nearly every day and at night our neighbor Mrs. Penney has had him over sometimes, but I know he has not had enough to eat and has never been much of a hand to cook. He has tried every Restaurant in Kirkland for his evening meals but you know how such places are . . . everything tastes alike.

Do not worry about us. We are doing famously and I have been a very good patient, no temperature except for the first few days. Perfect digestion. No complications of any kind and I have no Cancers or Tumors or any such tendency.

Did you get your two-story Chicken House finished?

Love to you all from
Mamma

A few years later Hazen wrote to his daughter . . .

The little hollow near the back steps is full of water this morning showing there was heavy rain last night . . . clearing this afternoon.

We are about as usual, which means I am just about worthless. We still have the boy come every second day but fearing that he was not coming Mama and I got in enough wood to last through tomorrow, but he came just after it got dark. Mrs. Penney came in, too, as the day waned and cheered us a bit. The coldest morning has been above 25 degrees ranging up to 52 degrees for the warmest part of it. The coldest weather was in the first half of November, but there will be frost tonight for it is 37 degrees at nine P.M. This is saying a plenty about our weather, but there isn't much else to write about. War news is too gloomy and dismal to write about and long before it is needed I fear you will hear much that is unwelcome and distressing.

Our love____

Dad
Geo. H. Pratt.

P.S. Looking for the shirt you sent me a year ago, Mama says she gave it back to you. You must thibk I am awful particular, but I intended to keep that shirt. Had a number of half worn out shirts which I wore this summer.
But never mind_____

Some time after this Emma wrote of her concern about Hazen in a letter to Dorothy. Dorothy, in turn told James of her concern about her father while they were eating breakfast one morning.

"I'm really worried about Dad, Jim. It isn't like him to quit working in that garden of his or even to take it easy at all," she said as she sipped her coffee.

"Well, maybe you'll have to go out there to see for yourself," James replied.

Dorothy was shocked at his response.

"Really? Go to Seattle?"

"Best way to see for yourself what's going on. Maybe your mother is just imagining things . . . and then again . . . maybe something serious is going on."

"Can we afford it?" Dorothy asked.

"We'll figure something out."

"Oh, Jim, you are so good to me."

She got up from the table and went around to hug her husband.

By this time in their lives together James and Dorothy, with their family, had moved from Chicago to Coopersville, Michigan to a piece of farmland James had acquired through his various real estate transactions. It was during the depression years. James and Dorothy lost their house in Chicago, hence the move to Michigan. They were devastated then to find that James' insurance company would only partially honor his policy because, they said, James had moved his family out of the state of Illinois. The monthly money he received was a bare portion of what he had thought it would be. It was definitely not enough for them to live as he had planned. He appealed again and again but was denied. It soured his entire life from then on. James became a disillusioned man. He was never the same person he had been before.

That is why Dorothy was so surprised to hear James when he suggested she go to Seattle to find out what was happening with her parents.

There was a grand scurrying around to get Dorothy ready and for her to brief the children, some of whom were now adult. James, Jr. had graduated from Lane Tech in Chicago, gone on to a good job and was already considering marriage.

George had one more year before graduation . . . and not too happy to have to attend the small town of Coopersville's High School for his last year.

Edward came somewhat reluctantly, too, but soon made friends of the neighbors and met a young girl named Faye with whom he spent quite a bit of time . . . with both Faye and her family. Edward fitted into the community quite happily but still he wanted a Lane Tech education. He started high school in Coopersville and worked hard on his father's farm, always doing as he was told. During the winters he went to Chicago and lived with his Aunt Isabelle and attended Lane Tech. Summers found him back in Michigan. After graduation his father insisted Edward had to stay and work on the farm . . . which he did. However, the very day of late April that he turned twenty-one he left Michigan and went back to Chicago. George was living with Aunt Isabelle and going to school. The two brothers became close, both coming to Michigan in the summer. They were at the farm when their mother set out on the train for Seattle. They worked the farm for their dad plus lending a hand sometimes to their sister Dotty in the big job she had inherited of cooking and keeping house for her dad and three brothers while their mother was gone.

When Edward left the farm it left only youngest brother John alone with his father James . . . James who kept insisting John work on the farm and do nothing else. John broke under the pressure and spent the next twenty years in a mental hospital in Michigan.

But, this story is not to be about the Randell family. This is Emma's story . . .

Dot . . . Dorothy . . . took the train to Seattle and wrote home to the family . . . "Had no trouble getting here. Asked "information" at the R.R. station. She was a lady from Chicago. She showed me where to get the bus and then I transferred to another one, which brought me to the ferry. Missed it by three minutes and had to wait an hour & fifteen minutes for the next one. Took a taxi to the house and got here a little before eleven. Ed's picture was smiling at me and Jack is looking at me from the top of the desk. They have many of my water colors framed."

Dot had left the Seattle area as a little girl so many years before that she couldn't have remembered much of how everything looked nor how to get around other than the ferry.

She wrote of her parents, "Mama has been in hospital since Monday night and they say she is holding her own though this a.m. her pulse was not quite so good. I am going now to see her during afternoon visiting hours.

"Dad was shaving when I arrived and he just stood & trembled so hard I was afraid he would fall over. They have been counting the hours 'til I came. A cousin of Mammas has been here since Thursday night. Dad went to the hospital too as he had to have meals so stayed right there until Thursday when this cousin came. She is about 6 years older than I."

In a later letter Dot writes, "Dad says to tell you the candy hit the spot. Mamma put it away in her suitcase at the hospital so she wouldn't have to give it all away. The doctor was here yesterday and brought some wheat germ vitamins to eat on cereal. He said Mamma came the nearest to passing out that anyone could. She had both doctors pretty worried about her for several days. Mamma says that she never was so sick before.

"Doctor has ordered digitalis once a day for Dad and is going to give him a sleeping capsule. He is to lie down 2 hours very afternoon. He coughs a lot which is now a bloodstained clot that he raises. The doctor thinks Mamma will be all right in a couple of months. But Dad can't stand anything. Too soon to talk about moving them."

In her June, 1940 letter Dot wrote several long pages of beautiful descriptions of a 152 mile jaunt that she and both her parents were taken on by the son-in-law of a good neighbor of Emma and Hazen. "Dad seems to stand the riding almost better than Mamma."

Dot stayed in Seattle for several months, but at last the calls and letters from Michigan had her back on the train headed east.

Chapter Twenty-One

*O*nce more it was Emma and Hazen together alone. It wasn't the same as before, though. Neither of them felt well. Emma fretted about her "love" as he was weak and frail, not able to work outside in their yard. He did well to get up, dress and be about the house without help. She didn't feel as sure of herself either . . . not as she used to. It was tough going.

One morning Hazen didn't come out of his room for breakfast as he usually did. Emma went to his room and opened the door cautiously. He was still lying in bed, apparently asleep.

"Mr. Pratt, are you going to sleep all day long?" she asked, walking into the room. She patted his shoulder gently with no response. She reached for one of his hands, which lay on top of the covers. It was cold . . . cold.

"Oh, Mr. Pratt, you can't go without me . . . you can't, you can't."

She threw herself down beside the bed, her head against Hazen's body, sobbing.

"Mr. Pratt, my love. How can I go on without you? No, oh no, no, no."

She continued talking to the forever-silent love of her life for quite some time, alternating between sobbing and talking to him. Finally, she seemed to come back to herself and realize that something had to be done. Although she dreaded being parted from Hazen she knew she had to call someone to help her.

At last she sat in the living room and flipped the pages of her phone book to get the number for the undertaker.

When Mrs. Penney saw the undertaker come and take Hazen away she came over immediately. She called the Whittenmeyers. When they came Witt called Dot in Michigan. Emma roused herself to talk to her daughter.

"No, Dorothy, you must not try to come out here again. I'll be all right. I have such wonderful friends and neighbors. I don't need a thing." She paused and listened for a bit.

"Your papa and I made our plans for this and arrangements are all made. He is to be buried in the

Kirkland cemetery. We already have a plot there. You shouldn't leave your family again this soon. I am so grateful you came to see your papa when you did."

Emma kept talking and talking to her daughter, finally convincing her that she didn't have to come to Seattle.

Although Hazen had purchased the plot some years earlier, now Emma had no money for a headstone.*

After she hung up the phone Emma went into Hazen's bedroom and began taking clothes from his closet. She laid his best suit out on the bed along with a clean white shirt, one of the pretty ties Dot had sent through the years, sox and clean underwear.

"There, Mr. Pratt. You are going out of this world dressed in your best." She nearly began crying again but closed her eyes, determined to not break down.

The next day with the help of Mrs. Penney and Mrs. Whittenmeyer she continued sorting Hazen's belongings. She found a good-sized box in which to put what she felt were the best of his things.

"I'll send these to Dot's boys. Maybe they can use the extra clothes," she murmured, more to herself than to her friends.

---

* It was some thirty years later that two of Hazen's grandsons, George and Edward Randell, bought, and had installed, a headstone for his grave.

Later in the evening Emma found two clippings of poems among Hazen's papers as she continued going through things. The first little love poem brought tears to her eyes as she read it.

> When thou art near me,
> Sorrow seems to fly,
> And then I think, as well I may,
> That on this earth there is no one
> more blessed than I.
> But when thou leavs't me
> Doubts and fears arise
> And darkness reigns,
> Where all before was light.
> The sunshine of my soul
> Is in those eyes,
> And when they leave me,
> all the world is night.

"How true. How true," she murmured as she read it again.

The second poem she found Hazen had saved was about his fondly remembered Vermont. She treasured it as she treasured all of his things and read both poems often to herself.

Vermont Freestones[*]

Daniel L. Cady, in "Rhymes of Vermont Rural Life."

If you are anybody's wife
You've heard of freestones all your life;
If you're Green Mountain born and bred,
You've took 'em both to church and bed;
You've still a stock on hand, no doubt,
A few with bails and some without;
A little one that fits your hand
And others upright, square or grand.

On nights when freezing breezes blew
What else would warm a bed 'way through!
What else induce the younger stock
To go upstairs at seven o'clock!
The jumping toothache knew their power
And "eased right off" inside an hour;
Tic-dollaroo refused to play
When freestones had the right of way.

Our folks had ticken covers made
For two of ourn, all bound with braid;
One stone laid still by grandma's chair,
And one we carried everywhere;
It fit right down inside the sleigh
And made our feet believe 'twas May_____
That stone and two good buffaloes
Let the chillblains hunt for colder toes.

---

[*]   Definition of freestone - rock that can be cut easily in any direction, in particular a fine-grained sandstone or limestone of uniform texture.

But now hot-water bottles splurge
As though they felt the cosmic urge,
And drool their drip along the path
From every sleeping room to bath'
You can't get sick and can't get well
Without that warmed-up rubber smell;
Go find the mattress__take week__
That hasn't felt a bottle leak..

Another thing about as bad
Is this new-fangled warming pad;
Who wants a wire from overhead
A-dangling down inside his bed?
Who wants along beside his form
A greenish fuse to keep him warm?
Besides, a charged electric wire
Might make your couch your funeral pyre.

So here I'll end as I began,
A strong, unbiased freestrone man;
The native stone that can't be beat
For parlor stoves or holding heat'
And when you're near to Perkinsville
Some day, jest ask 'em, if you will,
What 'tis about the freestone trade,
For that is where they all was made.

The love of Emma's life . . . George Hazen Pratt

IN THE NAME OF GOD, AMEN.

I, George H. Pratt, being of sound mind and body, do make my last will and testament.

I give, devise and bequeath to my beloved wife, Emma E. Pratt, all my property, real, personal and mixed, of every nature and kind whatsoever of which I die possessed.

And I do nominate and appoint the said Emma E. Pratt my executrix, to serve and qualify without giving any bond or surety as such executrix.

IN WITNESS WHEREOF, I do hereunto set my hand and seal this 28th day of September, A. D. 1921, in the presence of those who, at my request and in my presence, and in the presence of each other, have subscribed their names as witnesses to the signing, sealing and publishing of this will and testament.

GEORGE H. PRATT (SEAL)

Signed, sealed, published and declared as and for his last will and testament, by the said George H. Pratt, in the presence of us, who, in his presence and in the presence of each other, and at his request, have subscribed our names as witnesses thereto.

ELLE E. MALEN

JAMES J. BARBOUR

Chapter Twenty-Two

*N*ow it was just Emma alone in their little home, surrounded by its flower beds and shrubs all planted and once cared for by Hazen. Everywhere she looked she was reminded of him, of his not being there with her anymore. She scurried around trying to keep up with things on her own, but it wasn't long before weeds invaded flowerbeds, grass became too high . . . the list was endless. She continued hiring the young boy Hazen had called to mow the lawns; she weeded some herself, then was surprised to find a neighbor or two coming over to help her weed. It wasn't long before things began to look better, she was attending her club meetings and life was back as usual.

No. Life was not back as usual.

Life would never be the same again.

Emma forced herself to look at it as a new life. She attended the meetings of the Woman's Club and the Garden Club she belonged to, which kept her active and fairly content. But, gradually, gradually the relatively small amount of money left to her by Hazen was gone. She was reluctant to sell the stocks he had purchased in Illinois, as the interest from them was all the income she had now. What else could she do? She began selling the furniture she and Hazen had acquired throughout their years together. When this happened her friends became alarmed and finally Mrs. Penney herself called Dot in Michigan to tell her what her mother was doing.

This time there was no question of it being Dot's choice of the luxury of a trip to Seattle. This time she had to go.

Dot convinced her mother to come back to Michigan with her. Then, together Dot and Emma organized things. They packed linens, Emma's clothing and readied a few pieces of furniture for the movers. The rest was sold and finally, the house itself was put up for sale.

The vast changes in her life challenged Emma. At times she felt perplexed and confused. What am I doing, she thought, looking around her at what was left of her life with Hazen. I can't leave here. I can't leave him. No, no, I can't!

Dot saw her mother's bewildered expression and could understand how she was feeling.

"I know it's hard, Mother. It's like you're leaving Dad here, too, as well as your home." She put her arm around her mother.

"I hear you, dear . . . you're such a good daughter . . . I know I have to do something. I can't afford to stay here, but . . ."

She looked around, "It's not easy."

She reached back into the memories of her life and to herself she said, 'I will have to carry him with me in my heart . . . just like Papa taught us to do with Elizabeth so many years ago in Salt Lake City.'

The tears in her eyes spilled over and ran down her weathered, wrinkled cheeks. Dot put her arm around her mother again and squeezed her shoulders.

Emma dried her eyes and smiled at Dot, "I appreciate your help."

After Dot had moved her mother to Michigan she penned a small paper on what Vermont meant to her. In a way it was done for her papa as well as herself.

Vermont

I was putting fresh paper lining in a drawer in the highboy and there came over me a longing for a visit in dear old Vermont. I must be getting to the age where memories are a real part of one's daily living. I could see the highboy in Aunt Lizzie's front hall . . . hear the tinkle of the cowbell in the mistiness of early morning before the sun has lifted the fog from the hillsides. Soon, like a golden floodlight, the sun will shine on the scarlet of maple leaves, the gold of birches, the vermillion of sumac near the roadside, the dark green of scattered pines, the red and yellow of ripening apples among the still green leaves and the dark blue of grapes hanging high from a shade tree where the clinging vine reaches toward the sun.

The tingle in the air awakens one's zest for action and gives the needed pep for the days' labor in the orchard. With the picking of each fragrant apple, work becomes a game. Now in the warmth of mid-day one surveys the beauty of the far-reaching hills from the top of a ladder in a red Astrachan apple tree. Surely autumn is a glorious setting for the gathering of the harvest, and one's heart floods with thanksgiving and love for a heavenly father who has provided so much for the needs of the body and soul.

As we enter the house for dinner the sweet stimulating odor of grape jelly gives promise of that delightful treat of homemade bread and jelly. Cousin Elizabeth is very fussy about the proper amount of quiver each glass shall have and we know each one is fit for kings. We are happy just to be a part of an October day on the hillsides of New England.

Life in Michigan with Dot and James was an enormous change for Emma. She tried valiantly to adjust; she offered her help with the cooking and housekeeping, but Dot insisted her mother rest and take life easy. She did, occasionally, have Emma shelling peas or sometimes peeling potatoes or carrots in an effort to make her feel useful.

In the move Emma had packed Hazen's numerous diaries that he had so faithfully kept through the years. She read them over frequently feeling close to him again. She even tried to keep a diary herself but her entries were much the same every day, "Up at 8 o'clock, had breakfast. Cereal, two slices of toast . . . " But she did comment on the weather and quoted the temperature as Hazen always had in his diaries.

Emma read over Hazen's diaries frequently keeping them nearby in her dresser drawer. His letters, tied with a red ribbon were there, too. She honestly had no idea how she could have gotten through the days without the knowledge of his things there in the drawer in her room with her.

Emma did have some good times with Dot and her family. The camera caught a few of them . . . one here with Dot, Jim and young John Edward . . . son of Jimmy . . . who was visiting Michigan that summer.

There is another snapshot, this one a bit humorous. It looks as if they are having a picnic in a grassy field. Someone is making them all smile.

"Jim . . . pour us a cup!" It looks like a happy group.

The years went by with Emma adjusting fairly well to the life of "live-in mother-in-law." She joined the family for church and other social activities, and Dot and James' friends soon became her friends.

She made other friends herself and life was as good as she could ever expect it to be without Hazen. It was good until she began feeling unwell. She couldn't put her finger on exactly what was wrong. Nor could numerous doctors. Her own doctor put her in the hospital several times and the last time he issued a terse report:

SILAS C. WIERSMA, M. D.

INTERNAL MEDICINE

604 HACKLEY UNION NATIONAL BANK BUILDING

MUSKEGON, MICHIGAN

TELEPHONE 2-3650

April 3, 1950

To Whom it May Concern:

Mrs. Emma Pratt has been under my professional care since March nineteenth. She is suffering from generalized arteriosclerosis, arteriosclerotic heart disease and arteriosclerotic encephalopathy with disorientation, loss of memory for recent events and arteriosclerotic kidney disease with uremia. She has a right ocular cataract and recent left cataract extraction, fracture of the left femur at the hip just above the greater trochanter.

Because of poor general condition she is bed ridden and in traction and if she lives will continue 6 to 9 weeks (average). The uremia is now stable and no longer increasing. She has very few oriented lucid moments and is totally unable to manage her own affairs, social, personal or financial. Recovery is most unlikely, partial improvement may temporarily occur but is not anticipated.

Silas C. Wiersma, M.D.

Sadly, it was Emma's last hospital stay.

She passed away on April 26th, 1950.

Emma was buried in Rosehill Cemetery in Chicago . . . miles and miles away from Kirkland, Washington where her beloved Hazen was laid to rest. It's sad they couldn't be together.

But they are.

They are . . . I'm sure.

Somewhere in the hereafter they are walking along hand in hand, laughing together . . . happy . . . happy.

Printed in the United States
By Bookmasters